THE GOOD COP

THE GOOD COP

Peter Steiner

This first world edition published 2019
in Great Britain and the USA by
SEVERN HOUSE PUBLISHERS LTD of
Eardley House, 4 Uxbridge Street, London W8 7SY.
Trade paperback edition first published
in Great Britain and the USA 2020 by
SEVERN HOUSE PUBLISHERS LTD.

British Library Cataloguing in Publication Data
A CIP catalogue record for this title is available from the British Library.

ISBN-13: 978-0-7278-8943-0 (cased)
ISBN-13: 978-1-78029-615-9 (trade paper)
ISBN-13: 978-1-4483-0232-1 (e-book)

All Severn House titles are printed on acid-free paper.

Severn House Publishers support the Forest Stewardship Council™ [FSC™],
the leading international forest certification organisation. All our titles that
are printed on FSC certified paper carry the FSC logo.

Typeset by Palimpsest Book Production Ltd.,
Falkirk, Stirlingshire, Scotland.
Printed and bound in Great Britain by
TJ International, Padstow, Cornwall.

THE ARGONNE, NOVEMBER 11, 1918

Sergeant Maximilian Wolf of the Sixteenth Royal Bavarian Infantry lost almost his entire squad the last morning of the war. It was announced the fighting would end at eleven o'clock. All they had to do was wait, keep their heads down and it would be over. The trouble was the Americans had lost a lot of men crossing the Meuse, and General Pershing kept attacking. He was going to teach the Germans a lesson. Mortars rained down on them in the trenches. And when that happened, the captain ordered them over the top.

Some of the men – schoolboys, really – had arrived the day before in clean uniforms. They didn't have fleas or lice or rotting feet. They had terror in their eyes. They lit cigarettes with shaking hands. Now they were dead.

Levi Adler, Maximilian's friend, was dead too. Maximilian and Levi had fought side by side for four years – first against the French and now against the Americans. Levi was dead and Maximilian was alive, and Maximilian couldn't say which of them was the lucky one.

Now it was over. Maximilian sat on the edge of the trench and ate his ration of black bread and sausage. He drank deeply from his canteen. The water was warm and smelled of sulfur. He smoked a cigarette. He took a small notebook from his chest pocket and opened it to the drawing of Levi he had made days earlier. The eyes were wild and full of life. He turned to a blank page, rested his helmet on his lap and the notebook on the helmet, and began to draw what he saw across the battlefield.

Soldiers from both sides climbed out of the trenches, tentatively at first, but then more confidently. There were a few cheers on both sides as the truth of the Armistice sank in, but most of the men walked around in silence. A crow was cawing somewhere. American and then German soldiers picked their way across the mud to find anyone still alive. The air smelled of ordnance and blood and shit.

During his four years in combat, Maximilian had been seriously wounded twice, not counting the gassings. Once, early on, a piece of shrapnel had torn open his cheek and temple just behind his eye. A year later, white phosphorus had burned his entire back into scar tissue and taken him out of action for three months. His back still looked like a slab of meat, white and gristly with ropey purple and crimson stripes. It never stopped hurting.

'Here's Hagen,' someone shouted. Maximilian nodded to show he had heard. Hagen was one of the new ones. Maximilian couldn't remember what he had looked like. It didn't matter. He didn't look like anyone now.

Maximilian took the Iron Cross from his chest. The captain had always ordered anyone with decorations to wear them. 'For the Fatherland,' he had said. Maximilian dropped the medal where he had dropped his cigarette and ground them both into the mud with his heel. He went to help bury Hagen, or what was left of him.

The next morning Maximilian cinched the Luger high around his middle and pulled his tunic down over it. He filled his pocket with bullets. What remained of the company fell into formation and marched off the battlefield in a column of twos. The Americans stood and watched them go.

They came to a road where the trickle of men became a muddy brown river. The captain called out the cadence from time to time, in that high Prussian trill Maximilian hated. The men ignored the captain and walked as they pleased, out of step mostly.

They passed ruined farms with the bloated carcasses of horses and cows lying about, their stiff legs pointing toward the sky. They walked through what had once been forest but was now shards of shattered wood lying among splintered stumps and churned-up earth. You could see what was left of a steeple in the distance. The town – Fleury – was badly damaged. What windows remained were shuttered. No one watched as they passed.

A skinny dog came out of nowhere. It ran up to one man after the other until someone dug into his pocket and gave the dog a piece of dry biscuit. The dog ran with them then. Someone else gave it a scrap of food. It ran up to Maximilian. He reached down and patted the starving animal on his trembling ribs. Maximilian found a piece of sausage in his kit and fed it to the dog. The dog licked his fingers. And as it did, Maximilian felt tears well in his eyes. *Thank God*, thought Maximilian. *I'm still in here somewhere.*

THE RIVER STYX

The soldiers crowded into third-class carriages: four men on a wooden bench meant for two. And when the seats were gone men squatted or sat in the aisles as best they could. Every car in the train was packed with men. Even between the cars, where you could see the tracks below, they crouched or stood, one on top of the other, their rifles between their legs, their kits on their laps or backs. There were a hundred men in a car meant for thirty. It was winter and there was no heat, but the air was stifling and foul. Before they had all settled into place, the train lurched into motion.

Maximilian sat jammed against the window. The man next to him looked old, probably forty. You could see where the rank insignia had been torn from his uniform. Tufts of white hair sprouted here and there on his head and cheeks; he had great black bags under his watery eyes. Almost as soon as he sat down, he was asleep. His head hung heavy on his hollow chest. His breaths were shallow and rapid. He had a rattling cough deep in his chest. He whimpered from time to time without knowing he was doing so.

There was little conversation anywhere in the car, mostly just the sound of coughing or sneezing. No one knew it at the time, but the influenza epidemic had begun. In a month, the old soldier beside Maximilian would be dead from the flu. And by the end of next year the flu would kill fifty million people, three times the more than sixteen million people that had died in the war. The flu would spread around the world as soldiers returned home from the Great War.

The rocking of the car, the slow click-clack of the wheels, sent Maximilian into a dreamless sleep. After an hour the train shuddered to a stop, blowing out great puffs of steam. The men were ordered off the train. 'It's going back,' the captain said. But the train didn't move. Some men smoked. Those who needed to took a few perfunctory steps in the direction of a small wood and pissed onto the tracks. After an hour or so they were ordered back on the same train and it moved out again.

Fourteen hours and five unexplained stops later, they arrived at the barracks above the Main River north of Würzburg. The vineyards in the hills were intact but barren. There was a cold red sunset over the Main. Maximilian and what remained of his squad (ten men; three had disappeared since they had left the front) were assigned a room, with two ruined metal cots, an empty filing cabinet, and one electric light hanging from a cord in the center of the room. There was an adjoining washroom with a long metal sink, three showers, and two latrines. There was only cold water, but everything worked.

After an hour Maximilian took his squad to stand in line in the field kitchen in the center of the parade ground. From a huge kettle they were given a steaming bowl of hot potato soup, a slab of black bread spread with *schmalz*, and hot tea.

The three men who had disappeared were deserters. But what exactly had they deserted? There was no longer a functioning German government, so there was no longer any authority overseeing the demobilization of the military. The army was functioning essentially out of habit, like a headless chicken running in circles because its body doesn't yet know it is dead. Commands still came down from above, established patterns were acted upon, but without either authority or purpose.

Maximilian knew that. The captain had said as much. 'We're feeding and housing the men because we're the Kaiser's soldiers. It is what we do.' But the Kaiser had fled to Holland long ago. They were nobody's army.

Maximilian knew it was only a few days, weeks at best, until the military collapsed in on itself. 'That won't happen, Sergeant,' said the captain as though it were up to him. 'Our mission now is to prevent a soviet government from taking over.' *His mission maybe*, thought Maximilian. In fact, the army broke up. Some just went home and some joined small private armies, so-called Freikorps, that took one side or the other. The captain ended up leading a group of fifty men with the fanciful name the National Freedom Militia. They fought pitched battles in the streets of Würzburg against members of the Workers' and Soldiers' Council which, in the absence of an established order, had taken over running the city.

Before dawn, Maximilian made his way to the edge of the city. He hitched a ride in a truck delivering hops to a brewery in

Munich. The driver had a picture of a woman and child dangling from his mirror. He looked Maximilian up and down. 'From the front?' he said.

'No,' said Maximilian, although his uniform and kit said otherwise.

'What was it like?' said the man.

'I don't know,' said Maximilian. They rode the rest of the way mostly in silence.

Maximilian got out by the Leinthaler Bridge over the Isar River. 'Good luck,' said the driver.

'Thanks,' said Maximilian.

A beggar sat on the sidewalk halfway across the bridge, a cup in front of him. He wore a uniform, and, as Maximilian drew closer, he saw that the man had no face. That is, there was a hole where his nose had once been, and his jaw had been shot away and replaced with a metal prosthesis. What was left were two large eyes of piercing blue with lush long lashes. You could tell he had been a beautiful man.

'Welcome home, *Kamerad*,' said the man, and his eyes smiled. His mechanical jaw moved up and down like the jaw of a marionette, but his speech sounded almost normal. He picked up a concertina that lay at his side and began playing. It was Schubert's 'Erlkönig', of all things. After the introduction, he sang the entire song. A father and his son are on horseback galloping toward home. The child cries out that the Elf King is trying to harm him. The father sees nothing but the landscape around them. But he still rides desperately, driven by his son's agony. They arrive home too late. '*In seinen Armen das Kind war tod* – in his arms the child was dead.'

'I have nothing to give you,' said Maximilian when the song had finished.

'Sit down for a while,' said the man. 'That's good enough.' He gestured as though he were offering Maximilian a chair.

Maximilian sat down beside him. 'Were you a singer . . . before . . .?'

'I was. The Bavarian State Opera. But now nobody can stand to look at me. What about you?'

'I'm an artist.' He took out his notebook and showed the man.

'Draw me,' said the man.

'What's your name?' said Maximilian, and started to draw.

Maximilian sat with Klaus for an hour. The sunshine warmed them.

'Don't be fooled,' said Klaus. 'Munich looks normal. But you're entering hell. This is the Styx.' He gestured toward the river. 'I am Charon. Of course, you're leaving hell too. Both sides are hell.' They both laughed.

'Wasn't Charon a ferryman?' said Maximilian.

'Oh, they built a bridge. They don't need a ferryman anymore. Be well, *Kamerad*,' said Klaus, and gave Maximilian his hand.

DAS NEUE DEUTSCHE BILD

Maximilian Wolf – no one called him Max except Inge – started each day face down on the sagging couch. Inge, his sister, rubbed salve onto his damaged back. He closed his eyes against the pain and listened to the sounds of the city – the grinding of the streetcar wheels, the deep chiming of the bells from the Frauenkirche, Munich's great cathedral. He counted. Eight o'clock.

Karl, Inge's husband, was dead, killed somewhere in France. She had thrown her arms around Maximilian and wept when he had shown up at her door.

'It's me, Ingelchen,' he said. But she could see that, as emaciated as he was. She pulled him into the kitchen and fed him soup.

'Stay with me, Maxi,' she said. 'You can stay with me.'

He slept on the couch.

Inge took in laundry. Every day she scrubbed other people's linens in the sink in the stairwell and hung the wash on a line stretched across the courtyard. Clean wash in the sunlight was pretty much the greatest joy she knew.

The new German Republic had written a wonderful new constitution, modeled on the American one, founded on hope and aspiration, guaranteeing full freedom and universal democracy. The trouble was the left wanted a soviet union, the right wanted a dictatorship, and the army General Staff wanted control. Then came the Treaty of Versailles with its humiliating terms. The military was mostly eliminated, or was supposed to be. Parts of Germany were torn off by Poland, France, Belgium, Denmark. They were like jackals tearing at the flesh of a felled beast. Reparations of a staggering sum were to be paid to the victorious allies. There was no choice: the German Republic had to sign the treaty and, in that moment, it signed its own death warrant.

Some veterans wore their uniforms around; Maximilian never did. He was tall and strong now. You could see that. And the scar along his cheek made you think twice. People let him pass.

He had worked for two months at a slaughterhouse leading

horses to their death. The work was day to day, and the pay was minuscule. Still, some days he was able to bring some scraps of meat home. Sometimes he even had a little extra to sell. The work ended once the animals ran out. He swept streets then, until the street-sweeping ended. What was the point of sweeping streets in an unraveling society? At the moment their district was controlled by Spartacists whose objective was to join the Soviet Union. They wore red armbands. Even with all their guns, everybody knew they wouldn't last. Not in Munich.

Maximilian and Inge survived. They managed at least one meal a day. This morning it was potatoes, turnips, and some red beans in a broth made with oats. Maximilian carried the dishes to the hall and washed them. 'Maybe today I'll find something,' he said. He put on a clean shirt and jacket and left to look for work. He went out every morning, threading his way through cold, barren streets, past armed men behind improvised barricades. They clutched their weapons and glowered at him as he passed.

At the District Municipal Office a new notice said a printer needed a part-time delivery man. When Maximilian got to the address, there were already fifty people ahead of him. Someone came out and announced that the job was filled. Nearby a baker was looking for a helper. That job was filled too. A small weekly newspaper was looking for a reporter. Maximilian knew nothing about newspapers or reporting, but he went to the newspaper office anyway. There were only three people ahead of him: two men and a woman. The woman had journalism experience, and the editor, a small, bald man with thick round glasses, offered her the job. 'I'm sorry,' he said to Maximilian. 'The job is filled.'

Maximilian was about to leave when he looked at that week's paper displayed along the entry wall. *Das Neue Deutsche Bild.* Maximilian turned to the editor. '*The New German Picture?*' he said. 'So, where are the pictures?'

The editor smiled. 'We can't afford a photographer. Or, for that matter, a darkroom. Are you a photographer?'

'No,' said Maximilian. 'But I draw.'

'Can you show me something?'

Maximilian was back in thirty minutes with his notebook. The editor turned the pages and saw soldiers in masks during an attack – you could almost smell the gas. There was a drawing of trenches in the pouring rain. Levi's face. Soldiers searching for their injured comrades. Dead farm animals. The starving dog. Klaus with his concertina. Armed Spartacists at a barricade waiting to attack. Hungry children. A dead body on the steps of a church. 'I can't pay you much,' the editor said. He named a sum, and Maximilian agreed that it wasn't much. But he took it. His job would be to wander the city and capture moments of life in Munich. 'Political life, preferably,' said the editor, Erwin Czieslow. 'But, then, everything is political these days, isn't it? Hunger, poverty . . . so, draw whatever you see.'

Maximilian went all over the city, drawing political rallies, beggars, city officials, barricaded revolutionaries. Erwin printed some of his drawings in every issue, sometimes as story illustrations, and sometimes as stand-alone pictures of the life they were all living.

One day Maximilian did a series of drawings of Orthodox Jews. When the paper came out the next day, three drawings of the Jews – one of the bearded patriarch in his caftan, one of his son and his wife, and one of the children with their mother – were featured on the back page over an article with the headline FOREIGN WAYS THREATEN OUR GERMAN REPUBLIC. The piece went on to say that Germanic values were rooted deep in the soil of the Fatherland. The new Germany needed a unified people to survive and endure. But the German nation and its new order were under threat from the terrible Versailles Treaty and the inhuman reparations it demanded.

Foreigners meddling in German affairs had caused the war that had cost Germany millions of young lives. The war had been waged to protect the wealth of Jewish bankers and politicians who were not Germans at all. They had profited from the war and had stabbed Germany in the back. Foreign influences were infecting German culture from within.

'If it bothers you so much, Maxi, why don't you talk to the editor?'

'Doesn't it bother you, Inge?' said Maximilian.

'No,' she said. 'Frankly, it doesn't. If anything, it doesn't go far enough. The Jews are behind everything that's wrong. They run the banks. They're behind the so-called treaty that's taken everything from us. They're not Germans. Who do you think is collecting the reparations? The Jews.'

'How do you know that?' said Maximilian.

'You just have to look around, Maxi,' she said. 'Open your eyes.'

The next morning Maximilian went to Erwin. 'In the war,' he said, 'I fought alongside Jews. They died for Germany, just like everybody else. They suffered like everybody else. A Jew saved my life.'

'Listen,' said Erwin, 'here's the situation. Detlev von Plottwietz, who wrote that piece, is our publisher and our major funder. He pays *your* wages. Without him, the paper wouldn't last another week. He has his own ideas, and every once in a while he likes to write something. I don't like his ideas either. But when he writes something, we print it. That's not going to change.'

DAS ALTE ROSENBAD

'Where are we going?' said Maximilian.

Sophie Auerbach was walking fast. 'A meeting,' she said. She glanced at her notes. 'German Workers' Party. They're meeting at a bar on Herrnstraße. Probably nothing, but let's see what they're up to.'

Sophie, the new reporter, had asked Maximilian to come along. She had been roughed up at one of these gatherings the week before; Maximilian would offer some protection.

'I'm an artist, not a bodyguard,' said Maximilian.

'Don't worry. You'll get some good drawings.'

Herrnstraße was deserted. The street lamps were mostly broken. Some paving stones had been torn up. The pavement was scarred black where a barricade had burned. Das Alte Rosenbad was marked by a faded sign with a rose on it. Several armed men stood by the door watching who went in.

Sophie and Maximilian passed through the small, empty bar. As they opened the door to the back room, they were met by a wall of sound and heat. The room was jammed, mostly with men. Every space was occupied. People stood packed against the walls. An argument was going on about who should lead their movement.

'We need a man who can stand the sound of gunfire,' someone shouted. 'A man who can get the rabble to shit their pants.' A roar of approval went through the crowd. 'What about the veterans?' someone else shouted. 'You've got to get the veterans.' The crowd roared again. 'Not the officers,' someone else shouted. 'Those assholes stabbed us in the back.' The room erupted into shouting.

The man up front banged on the table, and finally everybody quieted down. 'Here's what we stand for,' he said. 'Read it.' Some men passed around mimeographed pages. 'Spread the word about the new German Workers' Party. Our next meeting will be announced on signs and in newspaper ads.'

'Which newspapers?' someone asked. He was ignored.

'Listen,' the man up front continued, 'for too long, a small, self-appointed government elite has been in charge. They sent us off to war while they got fat and rich. Now they're getting fatter and richer. Eating steaks while we're starving. Anyone here getting rich?'

'No!' roared the crowd.

'They take care of themselves, these elites,' said the speaker. 'They don't care about you. Who *does* care about you? Nobody, that's who. Those bastards lost the war, *they surrendered*, but you're paying for their treachery. For too many years, foreign industry has gotten rich on the backs of the German workers. And now German workers are being screwed again. The banks? They're doing fine. The Americans? They're fat and happy. The French? Oh la la. And the Jews? Well, nobody's doing better than the Jews.'

The crowd roared.

'The government says, "The people govern." Really? It's strange, don't you think? We the people have been in charge since the war ended, and no one has ever asked for our opinion. Not once. Treaties were signed that will cripple us for centuries. And who signed the treaties? The people? No! The November criminals did, which one fine day was the government just because they *announced* they were the government.

'This can't go on. *This must not go on.* They don't care about you. You and I – *we* have to put a stop to it. *We have to rule ourselves. And we have to protect ourselves.* "From whom?" you ask. Isn't it obvious? From the foreigners and the Jews who have infected Germany, who have destroyed German industry, who are destroying German society.

'We are going to take Germany back. We are going to start winning again, winning like never before. We will rebuild our industries. We will bring back our jobs. We will win back our Fatherland.

'We will build new roads and highways and bridges and railways all across this great nation. We will rebuild our economy, and we'll do it all with honest German labor.

'We can do it if we stand together. The bedrock of our politics will be a total allegiance to Germany. When Germany is united, Germany is unstoppable.'

The crowd stamped their feet and whistled and roared.

SOPHIE

S ophie turned the pages of Maximilian's notebook. 'These are good,' she said. 'Really good. This guy looks like a maniac. Do you think Erwin will publish this?'

'So far he's published pretty much everything I've showed him.'

'This is different,' said Sophie. 'Von Plottwietz, the publisher, is behind these guys, you know – this German Workers' Party. They're his boys; he's given them lots of money. He hates the Weimar government, hates the socialists, is terrified of the Bolsheviks. So if he's behind them, *the paper* is behind them, or will be before long. Don't show Erwin this one.'

'Why not?'

'You have to protect yourself.'

'From what? They're just drawings.'

'No, Maximilian, they're not just drawings,' said Sophie. 'They're hand grenades.'

'What about you?' said Maximilian. 'What are you going to write? How are you going to protect yourself?'

'I'll report what happened. What was said. I'll say how many people were there. I'm a reporter. No opinion, just the facts. I'll write about the guy that talked, repeat what he said . . .' She looked through her notes for his name. 'Hitler, Adolf Hitler.'

'So you feel all right writing what he said?'

'It's my job. I'm a reporter.'

'Will you report what he said about the Jews?'

Sophie set down her glass and studied Maximilian's face for what seemed like a very long time. 'Are you a Jew?' she said.

'No,' said Maximilian.

They were in a tea room not far from the paper. 'Why did you do those drawings of Jews? Why did you give them to Erwin?'

'They were good drawings. I didn't know he was going to use them that way.'

'Did you say anything to him?'

'Yes. Now I keep certain drawings to myself.'

'You're right. You should. Be careful what you show him. He's a good guy, but he's caught in the middle.' She reached across and touched the scar by Maximilian's ear. 'How long were you in the war?'

He took her hand away from his cheek. He didn't answer.

'My husband was killed in 1917,' she said.

'I'm sorry. He died for the Fatherland,' said Maximilian. It was what you said, even when you didn't believe it. *He died for the Fatherland.*

'How old are you?'

'Twenty-four,' said Maximilian.

'You seem younger,' she said. 'Except for your eyes.'

They sat in silence for a while.

'Everybody said he was a hero,' said Sophie finally. 'The pastor, his family, the officer who came and told me he was dead. They all said he was a hero. But he wasn't a hero. He was just an ordinary guy. He was cannon fodder. He was sent off to die for nothing. Nothing.'

'He died for the Fatherland. The Fatherland is not nothing.'

'No, you're right. The Fatherland is not nothing. But that war was not for the Fatherland. It was for power and influence and greed.'

'Don't you want to make Germany great again?' said Maximilian. She couldn't tell if he was serious.

'It's not *what* they want to do that's the problem. It's *how* they want to do it. Germany *was* great, because we have great scientists, great thinkers, great artists. But these guys with their slogans – Germany first, make Germany great, the German Workers' Party – they want to make it great the way the Huns were great, the way Genghis Khan was great. For them greatness means vengeance and violence, intimidation and fear.

'They want military and industrial power first of all, so they can punish somebody for whatever injustice they think has been done to them. They feel humiliated, ridiculed, and abused. All their talk is about hate and force and destruction. It comes from a dark place.'

'Do you have children?' said Maximilian.

'No children,' said Sophie.

'How long were you married?'

'Five weeks. I'll never have children.'

'You can't?'

'I *won't.*'

'Because your husband is dead?'

'His name was Johannes,' said Sophie.

'Because Johannes is dead?'

'Because Germany's not a place for children. Because Germany is in ruins and won't recover. It can't recover.'

'Yes, it can,' said Maximilian. 'Recovery will be difficult, but we can recover. We were stabbed in the back, sold out by the socialists in Berlin.'

'Do you really believe that?'

'It's what everybody says,' said Maximilian.

'Stop repeating what everybody says. It's just slogans. Look at who's saying it. You're smarter than that.'

'I don't want to argue with you. It's not something we can change.'

'That's true,' said Sophie. 'We can't change it. We can just report it and hope that the people change it.'

'How old are you?' said Maximilian.

'Twenty-five,' said Sophie. 'Going on a hundred.'

THE POLICEMAN

Hermann Gruber, a Munich policeman, watched the excited crowd leave the Alte Rosenbad. They had been whipped into a real frenzy by that speech. Hermann remained at the back of the room while the six men who had organized the meeting – the speaker was one of them – sat planning their next step.

Hermann was a realist. And he told himself being a realist meant that, when you see an opportunity, you seize it without asking too many questions. And here were maybe two opportunities at the same time. He recognized one of the men at the front of the room from precinct headquarters. Hermann was about to take the detective's exam for the third time. And he saw in this Hitler fellow a chance to advance his position in life. He had the sense that either Hitler or the other man, or maybe both of them, could definitely be of use. You never knew, but you had to take a risk if you wanted to get anywhere.

Hermann thought of his father and shook his head. His father had been a policeman too. But he had no ambition. And where had he ended up? Hoeing leeks and radishes in his small rented plot by the train yards. All he had to show for thirty-five years of foot patrols and night-desk duty was a tin medal for faithful service to the Kaiser and a pension nobody could live on.

The speaker, Hitler – Hermann didn't know his first name – didn't look like much. Thirty maybe, skinny, pale, a little mustache, dark hair combed flat. He could have been a concierge or a baker. Except when he spoke he had an explosive quality, an intensity that never left him. He had no patience for opinions; he was a man of the truth. *He just knew.* He had a sense of what was to come, and it was his destiny to force whatever it was into being.

'Gentlemen . . .' Hitler said, as though he were addressing the Reichstag and not this motley crew of would-be insurrectionists. At that point he noticed Hermann sitting back by the door. 'What do you want here?' he said. It was a command, not a question. 'We're working; the show is over.'

Hermann rose to leave. He gave a little bow in the group's direction and said, 'I admire your speech, Herr Hitler. I am with you one hundred percent.'

In fact, Hermann hadn't paid close attention to Hitler's speech. He had heard that stuff a dozen times. It was being spouted on street corners and in bars all over the city – the betrayal of the Fatherland, the dark times they were going through, the return of a mighty Germany. And the Jews, of course, were to blame for everything. It was always the same old political shit, to rope in the gullible and the naive.

But this had been different. The crowd of people weren't just persuaded. They were melded into one, lifted up, transported, and ready for action. The difference wasn't the speech, it was the speaker. Here was a man who, as someone had said, wasn't afraid of gunfire, a man who could scare the crap out of the rabble. Here was a man Hermann could hitch his wagon to.

The next morning, as Hermann came into District Headquarters to begin his shift, he saw the man he had recognized. Walther Reineke was a police captain and chief of detectives in the next district. Hermann saluted him. 'Herr Captain,' he said.

Reineke stopped. 'You were there yesterday, weren't you?' he said.

'Yes, Herr Captain.'

Reineke looked around to see who was listening. 'Come to the next meeting,' he said in a lowered voice. 'Then you'll really see something.'

'The German Workers' movement is a great movement, Herr Captain,' said Hermann. 'I want to be part of it.'

'Come to the next meeting,' said the captain again.

'I want to do more than go to meetings, Herr Captain. I want to be useful.'

'There are many ways to do that, Herr . . .'

'Gruber. *Wachtmeister* Hermann Gruber.' He saluted again. 'I am at your disposal, Herr Captain. I am at the Party's disposal.'

Reineke looked him up and down. He saw a man of average height with a barrel chest and a thick neck. His hair was cropped short and his lips pressed together in determination. 'Right now, Gruber,' he said, 'more than anything, we need foot soldiers. Men to put up posters, to patrol our meetings, to break Communist skulls. And we need men like you to recruit other policemen. That is something you can do right now. Remember: today's foot soldiers will be tomorrow's leaders.' Reineke put a hand on Hermann's shoulder. 'Come to my office in the Prinzregentenstraße after your shift.'

Hermann couldn't believe his luck. This Hitler was going somewhere. Reineke was his way in. And when it came to making detective, knowing Reineke wouldn't hurt either.

'Mitzi!' he called excitedly as he came through the apartment door.

He told her all about Hitler and Reineke and all the doors they would open. 'This guy is going to change the world,' he said.

'That's wonderful, Hermann,' she said. Hermann always came home with schemes that would make them successful or rich. And they usually went nowhere. She had heard it all before. This time would be no different. Hermann was eight years older than Mitzi, but she felt like the adult in the family.

FEBRUARY 24, 1920

S ophie and Maximilian found their way through the winding streets of the old city. The night was cold and snow was falling lightly. The bells of the Frauenkirche chimed seven-thirty just as they arrived at the Hofbräuhaus. The huge vaulted beer hall could hold over a thousand people. It was noisy and the heat was rising as others were arriving and finding places at the long oak tables. 'They can't fill this place, can they?' said Maximilian.

They sat down at an empty table just below the stage not far from a table surrounded by determined-looking men. They had on coats and jackets, despite the heat, under which there were probably knives, clubs, and worse. Their caps were pulled low on their foreheads and their faces stared forward in grim antici-pation. A great rosy blonde waitress in a dirndl put liters of beer on the table in front of them which they seized, clinked joylessly together, and drank from deeply.

By eight o'clock, the table where Sophie and Maximilian sat had filled up, as had all the other tables. People crowded onto benches wherever they could. The hall was packed. Most were supporters of the German Workers' Party, but there were also socialists and communists like the men at the adjoining table – communists, Sophie decided, whose purpose was to disrupt the evening and break some heads.

Finally a collection of Workers' Party officials filed onto the stage and took their seats behind the podium. Hitler was among them. Sophie didn't recognize the others. Johannes Dingfelder, an elderly doctor, was the first speaker. He read from a paper he had written about the historical origins of the current economic distress throughout Germany. 'In medieval Germany . . .' he began. A collective groan rose from the crowd. He was booed and jeered and heckled, but he went on with his speech to the bitter end even though no one was listening, finally shuffling back to his seat. Then Hitler rose and walked to the podium. He looked out at the crowd, then down as though he were embarrassed. He clasped,

unclasped his hands, shifted his feet. He passed one hand through
the shock of hair hanging over his forehead. He lifted his chin
and thrust it forward, gazing into the distance. He might have
been an athlete preparing for a race.

The crowd was slow to quiet down, but he began to speak
anyway in a soft voice that seemed almost gentle and was all but
inaudible in that vast hall. At first there were catcalls and hoots
of derision. Someone threw a bottle that landed not far from where
Maximilian and Sophie sat. A fight broke out. The men at the next
table shouted obscenities and shook their fists in Hitler's direction.
They swung their legs over their benches, ready to storm the stage.
But before they could even stand up, twenty men in brown shirts,
including Hermann Gruber, were on them, swinging beer mugs,
clubs, and fists. Similar fights broke out all over the hall. Those
who had come to disrupt the meeting were badly outnumbered.
After twenty minutes they had been driven from the hall, bloodied
and carrying their unconscious comrades.

Hitler had been speaking the whole time, laying out his Party's
platform. And as he spoke his voice had risen and had reached a
fiery pitch, as though he drew sustenance from the mayhem. The
pitched battles were his oxygen. He pounded his hand with his
fist and demanded a strong central government in Berlin. He wanted
nothing to do with this wishy-washy socialist republic. He jammed
his finger toward the ceiling as he promised that Jews would lose
their citizenship and all the rights that went with it when the
National Socialist German Workers' Party was in power (Hitler
had changed the Party's name). Everybody cheered. Many were on
their feet now. And the terms of Germany's surrender, that filthy,
deceitful Treaty of Versailles, would be torn up and thrown in the
trash. His voice became a shriek, a wail, an incantation that
seemed the direct expression of the collective will of the people
in that hall. His voice was their voice, his will their will. And his
greatness had become their greatness. They were cheering and
stamping and pounding the tables so that they couldn't even make
out his words. It didn't matter. Words didn't matter. Germany
would be great again. The crowd erupted and spilled into the
streets. Crowds of men, many of them drunk, swept this way and
that, breaking windows and beating up passers-by.

Sophie and Maximilian rode in stunned silence on the platform
at the back of the streetcar. Even the streetcar was filled with

celebrants. They cheered, 'Deutschland! Deutschland!' as though they had just left a soccer match and their team had won. They laughed at nothing at all, just out of exuberance, in jubilation at having found something to cheer about. Their lives had been hard, but that was going to change. Someone had understood their sense of oppression and helplessness and confusion, and he was going to do something about it. Their wide eyes glittered. Yes, they were drunk, but their intoxication didn't only come from the beer.

'So, what do you think?' said a small man with glasses. 'Isn't he great? Hitler?' He looked up into Maximilian's face with a great, happy grin that, you could tell, was foreign to his face.

'Great,' said Maximilian.

The man took Maximilian's hand and shook it enthusiastically. 'Great!' he said and turned to someone else. 'So, what do you think?'

Instead of riding all the way home, Sophie and Maximilian got off at City Hospital and went into the emergency ward, where injured people – men mostly – sat or lay wherever they could find a spot, waiting to be attended to by the unprepared staff. Sophie interviewed some of the injured and some of the staff. Maximilian drew the injured with their heads wrapped in improvised bandages or lying on the floor with their arms over their faces, hurt and defeated.

Finally, exhausted, he and Sophie walked to Tristanstraße. 'What have we just witnessed?' said Maximilian.

'I don't know yet,' said Sophie. They both fell silent. She took his arm.

Sophie had a small room in a fourth-floor apartment. It was just large enough for a bed and a dresser, but it was cheap, and it suited Sophie. The rent included bathroom and kitchen privileges. Elizabeth Grynbaum, the owner of the apartment, was happy for the company. Her son, a German professor, lived across town with his wife. But his health was failing and he didn't visit often. 'My son is getting old,' she said.

Madame Grynbaum, as she liked to be called, still gave violin lessons. She was old and tiny and walked on thin bird legs with the help of a stick. But in defiance of her age and infirmity, she dyed her hair the color of raspberries. Whenever she went out, she wore a brooch that she had had made of her husband's one and only service medal. He – Leonhard Grynbaum – had been killed leading a cavalry charge in the Franco-Prussian War fifty years before.

Young people came to the apartment most afternoons, where Madame Grynbaum listened intently as they sawed away on their small instruments, murdering Bach and Mozart. 'That was excellent, Trude,' she might say. 'But wouldn't it be even better if you did it this way?' Then she would tuck Trude's violin under her chin and play. Rich, warm sounds would fill the room, even from the most inferior instrument, and Madame Grynbaum would sway and dip, almost dancing as she played. Trude would then try it again, and Madame Grynbaum would hold her shoulders and make her sway as she played. She would sing in her ear. And, in fact, Trude would play better than she had before.

All Madame Grynbaum's students, children of all ages, loved her. They inevitably improved under her patient and excellent instruction, and many went on to populate the violin sections of orchestras around the city.

Madame Grynbaum was fond of Sophie, and she had grown fond of Maximilian too since he had been visiting. That he sometimes stayed the night didn't bother her. He was quiet and unobtrusive. You never knew he was there. Maximilian was respectful of her, and helpful too, running to a shop for this or that, or doing small repairs around the apartment.

In truth, Maximilian was a little afraid of her. He hadn't spent much time around old people. His grandparents had died before he was born. They lay in family plots in the cemetery up toward the lake above Bad Stauffenheim where Wolfs had lived and farmed for generations. As a child he had gazed at the fading photos on the graves without any sense that he was connected to these people. Whenever Maximilian spent the night in Sophie's narrow bed, it was Sophie who rubbed salve on his back in the morning.

DETECTIVE GRUBER

Willi Geismeier looked up as Hermann Gruber came into the squad room carrying his kit. So this was his new partner. The two men shook hands, and Willi pointed Hermann toward a desk by the door. Hermann put his box on the desk and looked around.

Willi was tall and thin, with thinning hair and thick glasses that made his eyes look tiny. He wore ill-fitting wrinkled suits that were shiny at the knees and elbows. His shirts were often untucked or had ink stains below the pocket where his fountain pen had leaked. When his tie wasn't askew, you had the sense that he had tied it correctly by accident. His desk was a mess, like he was, covered with folders and envelopes and stacks of paper. On top of one stack were pages of photos, which he picked up and leafed through over and over while the newly minted Detective Hermann Gruber settled in.

Hermann spent the rest of the morning at his desk going through the precinct's Standard Procedures Handbook and the current case log. At twelve o'clock Willi said suddenly, 'Time for lunch.' They walked to Zum Schwabinger Bach, the *Gasthaus* around the corner. 'One pea soup and *Bratwurst*,' said Willi to the waitress, 'and a half liter of Hofbräu dark.'

'The same for me,' said Hermann.

'Who's this then, Willi?' said the waitress.

'Hermann Gruber,' explained Willi. 'My new partner.'

'I'm Elsa,' she said with a smile, and shook Hermann's hand.

'The canteen is cheaper,' said Willi when she had gone. 'But sometimes I like to eat out. Just for a change.'

'She's pretty,' said Hermann, watching Willi for a reaction. He got none.

Hermann put brown mustard on the sausage in his soup and cut it in pieces. He ate a spoonful of soup and sausage and sipped his beer. 'This is good,' he said. 'So, how long have you been a detective?'

Willi explained he had been a rookie detective before the war.

Then he had spent a year in the trenches near Ypres in Belgium until a gas attack damaged his eyes and left him unfit for combat. He had spent the next three years in military intelligence, coding and sending messages. After the war, the police had taken him back, but on probation, as though he were just starting out.

Then Willi said, 'What's your story? How did you get here?' Hermann explained his years as a patrolman and that it took him several tries to pass the detective's exam. Hermann did not admit that he might have had help from Captain Reineke or that he was counting on a quick promotion.

'Was your father a cop?' said Willi.

Hermann said he was.

'I thought so,' said Willi, but he didn't say any more about that. 'Let's get back.'

Willi showed Hermann the folder for the case he was working on: weapons and ammunition stolen from a government armory. Someone had attacked the oak and iron door to the arms room with sledgehammers and crowbars. They had left the tools behind. But Willi suspected it was an inside job and the damage and the tools were for show – someone with access to the arms room trying to make it look like a break-in.

'What makes you think so?' said Hermann.

'First of all, how did they get into the building? Then, look at the photos. Doing that kind of damage would take a long time and make a tremendous racket. The guards do their rounds every hour. They would have heard something.'

'Maybe it was the guards themselves.'

'There are six guards all together. The two night guards are both recent hires.'

The night guards had been interviewed once already. They had reported the break-in. They didn't seem surprised to see the police again. Willi pulled them aside one by one and asked them to explain their routine, what they remembered from the night of the theft, how and when they made their rounds. There was no disparity in their separate accounts. 'Take us through your rounds,' Willi said. 'Don't leave anything out.' He and Hermann followed them up and down the halls, up and down the stairs. Their steps rang as they walked through the empty corridors.

'If someone was banging on the door here with a sledgehammer, wouldn't you hear it upstairs?'

'Not necessarily,' said the guard.

'What would it depend on?' said Hermann.

'I just don't think you would hear them,' said the guard. 'It's a long way away and on a different floor.' Willi had Hermann bang on the damaged door with a hammer while he listened upstairs. He couldn't hear a thing.

'How would someone get past you to break in down there?' said Willi to the guards.

'They couldn't. We're stationed at the only way in. One of us is always here.'

'And how would someone get sixteen carbines, two machine guns, and six boxes of ammunition past you and out of the building without being seen?'

'They couldn't,' said the guard again. 'Maybe they're still in the building.'

'What do you mean?' said Willi.

'Well, there's a lot of keys floating around here. And this is an armory with a lot of rooms. Many of these guys have access to different rooms, rooms that aren't used. They could have moved the weapons there, and then taken them out of the building little by little or at times when no one would notice.'

'Is that what happened?'

'I'm just saying, it *could* have happened that way. I don't know what happened.'

'But what makes you say that?'

'Look, I've only been here six months. I don't want to get in trouble and lose my job.'

'We need to see who has entry to what rooms. There must be some logs showing who has what keys. Who would have those logs?'

'You'll have to get authorization from the security officer to have access to those logs.'

'Who would that be?' said Willi.

Back at the desk the guards looked through the organization manual. 'Captain Steifflitz is the security officer.' Hermann filled out a request to interview Captain Steifflitz with regard to the key security for the armory.

They did not hear anything back, until one dismal, rainy morning. They were each looking over other, less urgent cases with an eye to closing some files, when Captain Reineke came into

the office. He stamped his boots to shake off the water. He shook
Hermann's hand. 'Congratulations on your promotion, Gruber,'
he said. 'I see you're settling in.' He then shook Willi's hand.
'Geismeier,' he said, looking as though he just eaten a piece of
rotten fruit.

'Herr Captain,' said Willi.

'Gentlemen, we're closing the armory case,' said Reineke.

'Closing it, sir?' said Hermann. Willi didn't say anything.

'We've arrested the two night guards,' said Reineke. 'They've
confessed. They took the weapons and gave them to their
Communist confederates. They'll be tried and severely punished.
I just wanted to let you know and thank you for your excellent
work.'

'How could they close the case?' said Hermann after the
captain had left.

'You heard the captain,' said Willi. 'They solved it. They caught
the perpetrators.'

'Those two mugs?' said Hermann.

Willi didn't respond.

Hermann tried another tack. 'Do you think they did it?'

'I don't think one thing or another. The case is closed.'

THE EDITOR

'Damn it, Czieslow, I'm amazed I have to bring this up yet again.'

'I understand your concern, Herr von Plottwietz. But we're a newspaper, and Sophie Auerbach is a journalist. Her job – *our* job – is to report . . .'

'Her job, Czieslow, and *your* job, is what I say it is. You seem not to have noticed the times we live in. They don't call for journalism. What the hell is journalism, anyway? Some elite version of things, some shitty pretense at objectivity.

'The times call for leadership; they call for action. The old idea of newspapering is dead. Look at the *Münchener Post* or the *Morgenzeitung* or any of the other old papers. Nobody wants that Socialist claptrap any more. They're good for lining birdcages, that's all. We need action newspapers and that's what *Das Neue Deutsche Bild* is going to be: an action paper.'

'The public wants . . .'

'I don't give a shit what the public *thinks they want*. The public *needs* motivation. They need hope. They need to know that their suffering will end. They need to know their lot will improve. That Germany will be theirs again.'

Von Plottwietz stood up to go, and Erwin stood too. The publisher leaned across the desk and shook his finger in Erwin's face. His own face was now red with anger. 'Here's the long and short of it, Czieslow. Your little Miss Auerbach has one more chance to toe the line – *my line* – or she's gone. I don't give a shit how good a journalist she is. Is that clear?'

'Yes, sir,' said Erwin.

'And get rid of those damn pictures too. What is that shit doing in my paper? Just so there's no mistaking what I'm telling you, Czieslow, your neck is on the line. This is my paper, and, goddamn it, it's going to be the paper *I* want it to be. Or you're all out on the street, the whole sorry bunch of you.'

Von Plottwietz stormed through the newsroom. He stopped

by the door, picked up a copy of the latest paper, and looked
at it in disgust. 'Jesus Christ!' he said and flung it across the
room. It came apart in the air and fluttered to the ground in
pieces.

Maximilian was told the next morning that he would no longer
be working for *Das Neue Deutsche Bild*. 'It's von Plottwietz's
call,' said Erwin. 'I'm sorry. Your work is good, Maximilian.
Something else will come along. I'm sure of it.'

'Thanks for saying that,' said Maximilian.

In fact, something else already had. The week before he had been
approached by an editor at the *Münchener Post* who had seen his
drawings in *Das Neue Deutsche Bild*. The *Post* would pay double
what Erwin had been paying him.

'That's wonderful,' said Sophie. She could see he wasn't sure.
'Take it,' she said.

'What about you?' he said.

'What about me?'

'I like working together,' he said.

'I like it too,' she said. 'But don't let that get in the way.
Your drawings are wonderful. More people should see them.
And they will when they're in the *Post*.'

'I don't know if I like the idea of more people seeing my
drawings.'

'Why not?'

'Just thinking ahead. What's to come.'

'Don't think ahead,' she said. 'We'll find out what's coming
soon enough. Take the job.' He hesitated still. But von Plottwietz
had made the decision for him.

Von Plottwietz had been leaned on by Party members objecting
to Sophie's stories. Despite her claims to be 'just reporting the
facts', she had described their rallies as 'disorderly' and described
Hitler as a 'fanatic nationalist'. She had quoted other politicians
critical of his economic ideas and his anti-Semitism. 'Those are
the facts,' she said.

'There have been threats against you, against me, and against the
paper,' said Erwin.

'Threats?'

'Phone calls. Letters,' said Erwin.

Sophie agreed to allow Erwin to go through the story she was

working on. He began crossing out words and phrases. 'Not unruly
– an unruly crowd. Say enthusiastic. An enthusiastic audience.'

'So throwing bottles, beating up people is enthusiastic?' This
was the last thing Erwin heard her say before the office erupted
in a ball of fire.

THE INVESTIGATION

'Two dead,' said Hermann Gruber. He had been at his desk when the call came in. 'And three injured; one badly.' By the time Willi Geismeier arrived on the scene, the ambulance had left with the injured and the police had erected barriers to keep the public away. The firemen were rolling up their hoses. Upstairs a police photographer was taking pictures.

'A bomb?' said Willi, looking around. The windows were blown out; the furniture was mostly in splinters. Sheets covered two bodies on the floor. There was blood all over the walls and floor. 'What do we know?'

'That guy over there' – Hermann looked in his notepad – 'Walther Hinzig, a pressman, saw two men open the door and throw something into the room. He didn't see what it was. It was probably a hand grenade, judging by the damage. But he got a look at the men that threw it.'

Walther Hinzig sat dazed on the edge of a desk while being tended to by a uniformed policeman. He had been shielded from the blast by the typesetting machine, but he still had cuts on his face and body from flying debris. His shirt was shredded and he was covered with blood.

Erwin Czieslow was dead, as was a young messenger. Blood was seeping through the sheets covering them. Sophie Auerbach was in critical condition with serious head and body wounds. She had been taken with the other two injured people to the hospital. She wasn't expected to live.

Hermann went to the hospital. The two injured were able to talk, but neither of them had seen anything. Beate Kerner, the receptionist, had been at the back of the room, far from her desk. 'Otherwise, I . . .' she said. Her jaw began to tremble, and she pulled the sheet up over her face and sobbed softly. 'My God. Oh, my God.'

Ludwig Bieberbach was sure he knew who had done it. 'The Commies,' he said. 'They'll do anything to keep people from knowing the truth.'

'How many were there?'

'I don't know.'

'Do you know the perpetrator or perpetrators?'

'No.'

'Had you ever seen them before?'

'I didn't see them at all. How many were there?'

Hermann then spoke to a surgeon leaving the operating theatre.

'How is Sophie Auerbach?' he said. 'Is she going to survive?'

'I think she will,' said the doctor. 'She suffered a serious concussion. And other serious injuries, some damage to her lungs, maybe her liver. A broken arm, leg, and ribs, and many cuts and contusions. But the swelling in her brain is subsiding. It remains to be seen whether she will regain her sight.'

'When can I talk to her?' said Hermann.

'She's still unconscious. And that's best for her, at the moment. If everything goes well and she regains consciousness, I'd say three or four days at least until she can talk.'

'What do you think caused her injuries, Doctor?'

'Obviously an explosion,' said the surgeon. 'You know that already, don't you?'

'Were you in the war, Doctor?'

'I was. I was a medic and then a doctor.'

'And did you see such injuries in the war?'

'A mortar attack would cause similar injuries.'

'Or a hand grenade?'

'Yes, certainly.'

Back at his desk, Hermann wrote up a summary report. The next morning he went to Walther Hinzig to interview him. Walther was staying with his grown daughter. He was still in shock and had little to add to what Hermann had already heard. He couldn't remember much of anything. 'You saw two men,' said Hermann. 'Can you describe them?'

'Not really,' said Walther.

'How old?' said Hermann.

Walther didn't know.

'What did they look like?' said Hermann.

'Average, I guess,' said Walther. He kept looking around the room as though he were trying to orient himself.

'Hair color?'

'I don't know.'

'Complexion?'

'I don't know. Fair, I guess.'

'Who do you think would want to do such a thing?'

'I don't know.'

'Do you think it was political?'

'I don't know. Maybe,' said Walther.

The next day Hermann decided to go back to the hospital to have a look at Sophie Auerbach. She was in the intensive-care ward, separated by screens from the patients to the right and left of her. A man was sitting on a chair beside her bed. He was drawing her portrait.

'Who are you?' said Hermann.

'Who are you?' said Maximilian.

'Police.' Hermann showed his identification card.

'I'm Sophie's friend,' said Maximilian. 'We worked together at the paper.'

'By friend you mean . . .?'

'Yes.'

'You worked at the paper, but you don't work there anymore?'

'No. I just started at the *Münchener Post*.'

'Why did you leave the *Bild*?'

'I had a better offer from the *Post*. But before I could quit, I was fired.'

'Fired? Why?'

'The publisher didn't like my drawings.'

'Where were you at the time of the bombing, between two fifteen and two thirty, day before yesterday?'

'I was in the offices of the *Post*.'

Back in his office, Hermann looked over the case log so far and then added some notes.

'So, what have you learned so far?' said Willi, sounding not very interested.

'Not much,' said Hermann. He didn't like telling Willi too much. He had caught the case and he wanted to close it himself. After a while, though, Hermann thought better of it; Willi might have some useful ideas. Something was off, as far as Hermann was concerned, and he couldn't quite tell what it was. 'There's this guy, Maximilian Wolf, who worked for the paper drawing pictures. Except he was fired five days ago, just two days before the grenade attack.'

'You think it was him?' said Willi.

'He has an alibi.'

'Yeah?'

'He was at the *Post* talking to the editors. It checks out.'

'But you think he's involved in some way.'

'I don't know.'

'So something's not right?' said Willi.

'Well, you tell me. When I got to the hospital to have a look at the girl, she was still unconscious. And this guy, Wolf, was sitting by her bed drawing her picture. That's weird, isn't it? What kind of person does that?'

An artist does that, thought Willi. But he didn't say it.

BARON VON PLOTTWIETZ

Maximilian had learned about the bombing from the wire in the *Post* newsroom. When he got to the hospital, Sophie was already in surgery. Maximilian met the gurney as they wheeled her into the intensive-care ward fourteen hours later. They tried to make him wait outside, but he wouldn't leave her side, except to eat or to go to the toilet.

He was sitting by Sophie's bed when Willi showed up.

Willi introduced himself.

'I already talked to the police once,' said Maximilian.

'I know,' said Willi. 'If you don't mind, though, I have a few more questions.'

'Do you have any idea who did this?' said Maximilian.

Willi said he didn't. 'Do you?'

'I told the other cop I don't. He thinks I did it.'

'Right now I'm just trying to get the lay of the land,' said Willi. 'I'm very sorry to hear about Miss Auerbach. Is there any news from the doctors?'

'They don't tell me much,' said Maximilian. 'I'm not family, so they won't talk to me.'

'Does she have family?'

'No,' said Maximilian.

'Let me see what I can find out,' said Willi. He was back in a few minutes. 'The doctor says she's out of the woods. Her vital signs are good. There may be some brain damage. And there was damage to her eyes. They still don't know whether she'll be able to see. They say she'll be in the hospital at least two more weeks, depending on what they find when she wakes up. It could be longer.'

'They expect her to wake up?'

'Yes. You were in the war, weren't you?'

'Who wasn't?' said Maximilian. 'The Meuse.'

'Ypres,' said Willi.

'I heard that was bad,' said Maximilian.

'I saw your drawings. In the paper,' said Willi. 'They're good. Why'd they fire you?'

'They didn't like the drawings,' said Maximilian. 'Politically, I mean. Erwin liked them, but the publisher didn't.'

'Erwin?'

'Erwin Czieslow. The editor.'

'So, if you had to speculate, who would you say rolled that bomb through the door?'

'I have no idea.'

'Look, Herr Wolf, your work tells me you see what's going on around you. In fact, I wish I had your gift. Did you ever think of going into police work? It's all about observation, you know. Anyway, if you'd be willing to speculate a little, I'd love to hear it. If not, OK too . . .'

'Have you talked to von Plottwietz?'

'The publisher?'

'Yeah, him.'

'You think he blew up his own paper?'

'I'm not saying that. But he's involved in radical politics in a big way. Who knows? He might tell you something.'

Baron Detlev von Plottwietz lived alone in a spacious apartment opposite the State Opera. Though in the middle of the city, the apartment was furnished as though it were a hunting lodge, with heavy, dark furniture and the heads of boar and deer hanging above the fireplace. Across the room, facing the fire, was a full-length portrait of von Plottwietz in formal regalia. He had a large silver medal pinned on a blue and white silk sash.

'*Virtus et Honus*, virtue and honor,' said von Plottwietz, coming into the room. 'The Order of Merit.'

'I see,' said Willi. 'Congratulations. And thank you for seeing me, Herr Baron.'

'I assume you're here about the bombing,' said von Plottwietz.

'Yes,' said Willi. 'I'm sorry for your loss,' which was what you always said to start these interviews. 'It must be difficult for you to lose Erwin Czieslow that way, and to have Sophie Auerbach so terribly injured.'

'Yes, it is,' said Detlev. His face remained immobile. He motioned for Willi to take a seat and then sat down with the portrait above and behind him. 'Yes,' he said again. 'It really was quite terrible and unnecessary.'

'I won't take much of your time. You've probably had quite enough of policemen and our questions.'

'Not at all,' said Detlev with a tight smile. 'You're the first.'

'Am I?' said Willi, trying not to sound surprised. 'Well, I'll try to be quick. I really want to get your point of view on the entire affair and find out whether there's anyone you can think of that might want to do such a thing.'

'Well, it came completely out of the blue, a bolt of lightning. Terrible. Unimaginable.'

'You said a moment ago, this attack was "terrible and unnecessary". What did you mean by "unnecessary"?'

'Well, it didn't accomplish anything, did it? It won't stop our getting the story out about who's trying to destroy Germany and why they're doing it. And how we're going to annihilate them.'

'So you intend to reopen the paper?'

'Of course,' said von Plottwietz. 'And I guarantee you, we will be successful. Saving the Fatherland is my mission in life. A fair and honest German press is one of the indispensable means for saving the Fatherland and making it strong again. Getting the *real* truth out; disputing the phony crap the Bolsheviks print in their so-called newspapers.'

'Who do you think might have bombed your offices, Herr Baron? It sounds as though you might have your suspicions.'

'Suspicions? Well, Herr Detective, it seems obvious to me. When you get around to catching the perpetrators, I promise you they will be Jews, Bolsheviks, liberal-socialists – someone who doesn't want the truth about the current national government to get out.'

'So, not someone with a personal grudge. You would rule out any sort of personal attack?'

'Personal attack? Nonsense.'

'I see,' said Willi. 'I take it your newspaper is fully insured against events such as this.'

'Naturally. My attorney tells me we're fully covered. We will be up and printing again in no time.'

'So the attack doesn't affect you that much, personally, I mean.'

'Of course it affects me . . .'

'Could this have been a personal attack against one of your staff? Erwin Czieslow, for instance, or Sophie Auerbach, your star reporter, or Maximilian Wolf?'

'Herr Wolf no longer works for the paper. Get your facts straight, Herr Detective.' The baron was becoming impatient. 'Wolf was fired before the attack occurred.'

'Why was he fired, Herr Baron?' Willi had taken out a small notebook and was making notes. This caused von Plottwietz to look around, as though there might be something going on behind him he needed to be careful about.

'His drawings are terrible,' he said. 'Have you seen them?'

'And you don't suspect him of wanting revenge for being fired?'

'He's not man enough,' said Plottwietz. 'And Erwin Czieslow and Miss Auerbach were going to be terminated soon as well. Their work was highly unsatisfactory, unprofessional. They had become superfluous.'

'Have you chosen their replacements already?'

'I will edit the paper myself. And I'll use writers who understand and can tell the hard German truth.'

'I see,' said Willi. 'I see now why you seem so indifferent to Erwin Czieslow's death and Sophie Auerbach's injuries, as well as the suffering of the rest of your employees.'

Baron Detlev von Plottwietz stood up angrily. 'This interview is over, Detective,' he said. 'Get out of my apartment.'

But Willi sat a moment longer, finishing his notes, speaking to himself as he wrote. 'Indifferent . . . to death . . . tell . . . the . . . German . . . truth. Thank you for your time, Herr Baron. You have given me much to think about.'

DETECTIVE GEISMEIER

Back at his desk, Willi went through his notes. 'I talked to von Plottwietz,' he said to Hermann.

'Really?' said Hermann. He stopped what he was doing. 'Why'd you do that?'

'Well, it's his newspaper that was bombed. To me that would seem like the place to start.'

'Who's going to bomb his own newspaper?' said Hermann, trying to sound incredulous.

'People burn down their own businesses all the time, for the insurance or other fraudulent purposes. All the time.'

'Not the baron,' said Hermann. 'He was decorated by the King of Bavaria.'

'Oh, so you know him?' said Willi.

'I know who he is,' said Hermann. 'I did my homework.'

Willi rummaged through folders on his desk to remind himself what else was going on.

'So, what did you learn?' said Hermann after a while.

'About the baron? Nothing really,' said Willi.

'That's what I figured,' said Hermann, but he did not sound reassured.

'I'll be out for an hour or so,' said Willi after a while.

'Where are you going?' said Hermann.

'Another case,' said Willi.

'Which one?' said Hermann. But Willi was already out the door.

Maximilian was sitting by Sophie's bedside with a bowl of bouillon in his left hand and a spoon in his right. Sophie had a large cloth napkin across her chest. Her mouth opened slightly as Maximilian moved the spoon toward her. Willi watched from across the room for a moment. Her eyes shifted as Willi approached, causing Maximilian to turn to see who was there. He smiled at Willi. So, the news was good.

'Good afternoon, Fräulein Auerbach. I am Detective Willi Geismeier. I'm glad to see you are improving.' The bruises and cuts around her eyes were less angry than they had been. But her eyes were unfocused and half-closed.

'She woke up this morning,' said Maximilian.

'That's good,' said Willi.

'She's very tired, not ready to talk yet. The doctors say she needs lots of rest.' And, as if on cue, her eyes fluttered shut. Maximilian set the bowl aside and removed the napkin.

'Actually,' Willi said, 'I'm here to talk to you, Herr Wolf. Or rather to look at your drawings, if you'll let me see them.'

'My drawings?'

'Since the bombing.'

'They're personal,' said Maximilian. 'I'd rather not show them.'

'I understand,' said Willi. 'But they might help us catch the people who did this.'

Max gave him the notebook and Willi leafed through the pages, pausing when he came to a quick sketch of his own face. He stopped again at the portraits of Sophie.

'You know Walther Hinzig,' said Willi.

'The pressman?'

'How well do you know him?'

'Just from the *Bild* offices. A nice man.'

'Herr Hinzig was facing the door when the bombers came through. He saw them throw the bomb. When we first talked to him, he didn't remember anything about them. He was in shock.

'Now, I look at these drawings of yours, Herr Wolf, especially the faces: Fräulein Auerbach. And me. Particularly the picture of me. You drew that after we met for the first and only time. We spent maybe a minute together. And you drew from memory. And yet anyone could see that's me.' Willi shook his head in wonder. 'So, I'm thinking, if I could sit you and Walther Hinzig down together, you could show Walther a sketch and he could say, "No, the nose is more pointed," or "the eyes are further apart," and you could . . .'

'Don't you have police artists for that? Why not use one of them?'

Willi fidgeted uneasily on his chair. 'For certain reasons I . . . don't want to go into, *can't* go into, I want to do this . . . outside the department. And just between us – you and me and Herr Hinzig.' He watched Maximilian. He could see the wheels turning.

'So you think . . .'

'I'm not saying any more about it,' said Willi.

'OK,' Maximilian said. 'I'll do it if you think it will help.'

The next afternoon there was a knock on Walther Hinzig's door. His daughter opened it and Willi introduced himself and Maximilian. She led them to her father, who sat wrapped in a warm coat and muffler on the balcony looking across the street to a small park. Walther seemed baffled by Willi's presence. 'I already talked to the police,' he said. But when Willi presented Maximilian, Walther's eyes showed a glimmer of light.

'How are you doing, Walther?' said Maximilian.

'Not bad,' said Walther, and lowered his eyes as they filled with tears. Then he remembered Sophie and said, 'Have you seen Fräulein Auerbach? How is she doing?'

'She's getting better, Walther. She can see. Her wounds are healing. She just needs lots of rest. And then she'll have to go through physical rehabilitation.'

'Thank God,' said Walther.

'Herr Hinzig,' said Willi, 'I know you weren't able to identify the people who bombed the office.'

Walther dropped his eyes again.

'But I'm thinking an artist, like Maximilian here, might be able to help you dig out details that you don't even know you remember about these men. So, he could do a drawing based on whatever you *do* remember. Then you'd tell him what's right and what's wrong with it, and he'd correct it. Are you willing to try that?'

'I really don't remember anything,' said Walther.

'I know,' said Willi. 'But why don't we give it a try?'

'I don't know,' said Walther.

'It would be a big help, Herr Hinzig,' said Willi.

'Give it a try, *Vati*,' said his daughter.

'So what do you remember, Herr Hinzig?' said Willi. 'Start with either man.'

Walther pressed his eyes shut and thought.

'He was . . . average looking,' he said. He shook his head in frustration, but Maximilian started to draw. In a few seconds he held up a sketch of a generic man's face, the sort of face you might see in an advertisement for toothpaste or cigarettes.

'No, that's not him,' said Walther.

'How's the hair?' said Maximilian.

'There's too much hair,' said Walther. 'It wasn't wavy. And it didn't come to his ears.'

Maximilian rubbed out the hair and redrew it. 'Like this?'

'Yes, maybe. But his forehead wasn't that tall, or his eyebrows were, I don't know, higher up maybe?'

Maximilian drew.

'No, not that high.'

'Like this?'

'Closer together.'

Maximilian erased and redrew, and each change he made seemed to trigger a new memory. The ears were larger, the eyes were small and closer together, deep set. There were bags under them. The nose was snub so you could see the nostrils. There were deep wrinkles from beside the nose to the corners of the mouth. Thin mouth, open, downturned, strong cleft chin, large Adam's apple. Maximilian drew and redrew, and when the page became too smudged, he quickly redrew the last version on a clean sheet.

'That's him!' said Walther suddenly, astonished by what his suppressed memory had now brought to light. 'That's him.' The second man came to life even faster, and Walther was amazed all over again.

'Thank you, Herr Hinzig,' said Willi. 'That was outstanding work.'

'Wait!' said Walther, suddenly remembering something else. 'His hand!'

'His hand? What about his hand?' said Willi.

'The second guy's hand, his right hand. It was in a black glove. Like it was damaged or artificial. It just hung at his side.' Now Walther couldn't *stop* remembering.

'Do you know who they are?' said Walther.

'I don't,' said Willi. 'But I may know someone who does.'

THE GRAND SCENARIO

Putzi Hanfstaengl had learned how to throw a party during his student years at Harvard University. Now he oversaw the family publishing business in Munich, though, in truth, the business more or less ran itself. Putzi's main talent was still having parties, and he used that talent now to bring together his new friend Adolf Hitler and people who might be willing to give him money. The evening was chilly and there was a crackling fire in the fireplace. Putzi sat sipping champagne, chatting with various guests, and noodling on the piano. Baron Detlev von Plottwietz had met Captain Walther Reineke, a district chief of detectives, at one of Putzi's garden parties the previous spring. The baron was a bore, but a rich bore. The baron approached Reineke with a determined look in his eye. Reineke tried to maneuver away from him, but the baron was tenacious and ran him to ground in the library.

'Ah, Herr Baron, it's you. How are you this evening? Have you met Frau Doktor Bechstein?'

The baron had not met Frau Doktor Bechstein. Nor was he at all interested in meeting her. He clicked his heels and offered her a perfunctory *Handkuß*. Frau Bechstein gave him one up and down look, smiled sourly, and took the arm of someone who steered her away. Von Plottwietz had only one thing on his mind, and that was Willi Geismeier.

The next morning Reineke stormed into the precinct detectives' offices. 'Where the hell is Geismeier?' he shouted. Someone pointed toward Willi's desk. Willi had stooped down and was gathering together papers that had finally slid from the precarious stack to the floor.

'Geismeier, a word!' said the captain.

'Herr Captain?' said Willi, standing at attention.

'I'm taking you off the newspaper bombing.'

'Any particular reason, Herr Captain?'

'I want you to focus on open cases you've already got. For heaven's sake, look at your desk. Clear some cases, will you?'

'Did someone complain, Herr Captain?' said Willi.

'Why do you say that, Geismeier? What have you been up to?'

'Nothing, Herr Captain.'

'You're off the case – that's all there is to it. Gruber will take over. It's right up his alley. Right, Gruber?' He turned toward Gruber with a smile.

'Yes, sir!' said Gruber enthusiastically. 'It looks open and shut, Herr Captain.'

'Open and shut. There, what did I tell you, Geismeier? While you're out muddying the waters, Gruber is solving the case.'

'Yes, sir, Herr Captain,' said Willi.

'Come with me, Gruber. Bring me up to date on what you've got.'

When Reineke and Gruber had left the office, Willi dug into the pile of papers on his desk and found the folder with his notes from the bombing case. He leafed through the pages until he came to a peculiar schematic he had drawn.

Captain Reineke hated Willi Geismeier. Willi seemed to regard police protocols as bothersome inconveniences that were best ignored. Moreover, his personal appearance was disgraceful and his manners were appalling. The only problem was that damned clearance record of his. Since coming back from the war, Willi had closed more cases than any other detective in the district. Every month he was at the top of the list Reineke turned in to the chief of detectives. That was the only thing that kept Reineke from firing him.

Willi had not been born to be a police detective. His father, a prosperous factory owner, had expected his only son would go to university and then take over running Geismeier Ceramics. But on being granted his diploma in literature with high honors at Tübingen University – he had written a thesis on criminality in Shakespeare's plays, focusing particularly on Richard the Third – instead of joining Geismeier Ceramics, he had joined the police force.

To his father's credit, he recognized right away that Willi's particular brand of intelligence suited literary exegesis and, coincidentally, police work better than it did the manufacture of seamless ceramic pipe. And it didn't hurt Willi's cause that Benno von Horvath, one of his father's dearest friends, had spent his career as a police officer and then as a senior police official. 'I'll watch over the boy,' he said. But it wasn't necessary. Willi proved quickly that he was a gifted investigator.

Willi had learned from the English bard that lawful human behavior followed well-mapped social patterns. But every crime was a unique moment in human history, where human psychology and behavior ran off the rails in a very particular way. When you looked into crime thoroughly and deeply, as Willi had, it revealed dark, as yet uncharted corners of the human soul. Criminal activity oozed through civilization's unmapped dark alleys in ways that were surprising, illuminating, and, for Willi, irresistible.

Willi had developed his peculiar theory of crime and civilization over time. But his theory became reality in a flash in the savage trenches at Ypres. One gray winter morning – the sky had turned a metallic gray – his platoon was overrun by French soldiers pushing bayonets into every German they saw. Willi seized the machine gun and repelled the French attack with a ferocity no one would have thought possible of anyone, let alone Communications Sergeant Willi Geismeier.

His superiors wanted to recommend him for the Iron Cross. But Willi did not see himself as a hero and resisted mightily. In the end the Iron Cross went to someone else. Willi never spoke of the experience again. Instead of a story to tell or a medal to wear, Willi took from the experience a profound sense of the chaos that surrounds us. And in that same moment an intense desire to understand how that chaos found its way into civilized society. If he could understand that, he would understand crime.

Back in the police department, Willi set about developing methods, which he mainly kept to himself. Every crime had what he called a 'grand scenario', by which he meant not just the physical scene of the crime or the principal actors. He was interested in the relationships among *all* the players in the crime's universe: suspects, witnesses, and victims, of course, but also the individual police, detectives, judges, politicians, and bystanders who drifted on and off the stage and how they interacted with their surroundings. Even the society at large came into play. All these elements formed a fluid, shifting constellation whose dynamics could reveal things the ordinary search for clues and witnesses might leave undiscovered.

The Munich police department had always been nationalistic, with a strong connection to the army. And, like the army, they had always been insular and suspicious of civilian ways. Benno von Horvath, his mentor, was himself from a Bavarian military family. But now, in the expanding instability, not to say chaos, of postwar Germany the police had allied themselves more and more with dangerous and extra-legal elements: renegade political parties, anarchic movements and worse. Police higher-ups became involved in political schemes as they never had been before, and those who didn't were sidelined. With the police department changing as it was, Willi's grand scenario idea made even more sense to him than it had before.

Willi was certain that Captain Reineke was somehow involved in the armory robbery, and Gruber was just as certainly the captain's acolyte. Policemen like these now saw their mission as something other than law enforcement. Their job was not so much to prevent and to solve crime as to *use* crime to advance their political and personal agendas.

Willi drew a diagram for every case he was involved in – much as he had done as an undergraduate with Shakespeare's plays – which he kept in a private folder. In fact, he kept two sets of case files, a conventional one for his superiors in a department file drawer and another more thorough one for himself, safely hidden – either at home, or, if it was active, buried in the stack of papers on his desk.

Alone in the office, he unfolded the schematic for the newspaper bombing. The names of the players were arrayed around the page with a dizzying web of lines connecting them to the other players he had identified so far. Willi himself (W.G.) was on the chart, as were Gruber and Reineke. He had drawn a dotted line between the two of them. And now, thanks to his talk with von Plottwietz and Reineke's removal of Willi from the case, he could draw a line between the baron and Captain Reineke.

He drew lines from all three to A.H. further on the periphery of his schematic. A.H. stood for Adolf Hitler, about whom both Reineke and Gruber had spoken in admiring terms. He drew lines to the Bavarian General von Lossow in charge of the police as well. He felt certain Reineke was not freelancing.

Willi drew lines connecting Walther Hinzig, Erwin Czieslow, Maximilian Wolf, Sophie Auerbach with one another and with P-1 and P-2 – Perpetrators 1 and 2, the men whose portraits Maximilian had drawn. After a moment's hesitation he drew lines between P-1 and P-2 and Baron von Plottwietz. He was speculating here, but he would have been surprised to be proven wrong. He slipped the schematic back into his file, along with Maximilian's portraits, also labeled P-1 and P-2, at least until he had names he could attach to them.

THE PRIVY COUNSELOR

Willi was not fond of parties. But once in a while he showed up at the Horvaths' occasional Sunday evenings, to their delight and the profound puzzlement of the other guests, who were mostly doctors and lawyers and professionals of a higher sort. Willi was the only policeman, unless you counted Benno von Horvath. There were usually eighteen or twenty guests, although the numbers had recently dwindled some. The streets were more dangerous now, and people were reluctant to come out after dark.

On this particular evening, things began, as they always did, with a simple buffet dinner of cold sliced ham, sausages, and various cold salads. The wine was plentiful, and there was of course beer. Guests got their food and then sat here and there around the large drawing room, their plates balanced on their knees, their glasses somewhere within easy reach.

As it almost always was these days, the talk was about the faltering Republic, the various efforts to overthrow it, the rising power of the army, and of course the hated Treaty of Versailles. Adolf Hitler was still mostly unknown in the rest of Germany, but in Munich people had at least heard the name by now. His rallies were notorious and his pronouncements were alternately ridiculous and alarming. So there was curiosity and some sighs of puzzlement or exasperation.

'It's all too depressing,' said Margarete. 'Why do we even have to *think* about such awful people?'

A minuscule man with a goatee who wrote essays about politics spoke up. 'Don't dismiss him, my dear lady. He is a brilliant speaker, and, while he has unconventional tendencies when it comes to politics, he has a canny ability to arouse a crowd and turn them to his purposes.'

'So what?' someone else said. 'He's a thug and a liar, isn't he? Who's going to listen?'

'Well,' said the essayist, 'maybe. But you know how we Germans love a good speech. And, to tell the truth, despite some of the nonsense he spouts, he's got an interesting and not entirely wrongheaded point of view. For instance, at the moment *he's* not advocating Bavarian secession, as everyone else seems to be. He's calling for a strong central government. Of course, he hates the current government, as we all do,' said the essayist, checking the room, to make certain there were no dissenters. 'The "November traitors," he calls them, sold us out, and I tend to agree. He wants to defy Versailles and restore Germany's greatness. I think he has to be taken seriously.'

'Really? Taken seriously?' This was a prominent surgeon speaking. He wore tinted glasses and a tiny red, white, and black rosette on the lapel of his suit, which signified some military order or other. 'This Hitler's proposal, at least as you summarize it – I confess, I haven't followed him or any others of his ilk, but it sounds *very* radical, and, I must say, very unlikely. I mean, you're talking about a dictatorship, aren't you? OK, yes, the Berlin government is weak and unsure of itself. But, damn it, it has the army behind it. General Seeckt recently said as much. It was in the paper. The constitution is strong. It's a good constitution. And under the constitution, if things get precarious, the president can always declare an emergency and govern by decree. And, damn it, the army stands behind him.'

'Well, they do, yes, of course they do,' said the essayist. '*Now* they do. But for how long? Where will the army stand if the president caves in on the French occupation of the Ruhr, for instance, and continues to let the French cripple our mills and mines and factories and ruin our economy? Or what if the government decides to start paying reparations again? Where will the army stand then? Or what if the army itself is ever forced to disband properly as Versailles says it must?'

'And,' the surgeon's wife chimed in, 'I wonder where the army will stand when inflation really becomes impossible. Seventy marks to the dollar is one thing – bad enough when we were at five marks a year ago. But where will the army stand when it's seven *thousand* marks to the dollar and a loaf of bread costs two thousand marks?'

'Don't be ridiculous.'

'That will never happen.'

Everyone scoffed at the idea that inflation could ever reach such levels. But someone else pointed out that as long as the government went on printing money, inflation would continue, and could

go higher than anyone imagined, as eventually it did, rendering
the mark essentially worthless.

No, the army would certainly not stand by and watch forever.
The army was run by the Prussian warrior class. They were heavily
armed and were used to running things, as they had for the last fifty
years. True, it was the army that had surrendered, but they hadn't
had any other choice, had they? And they had nothing to do with
Versailles. That was certainly not their fault. That was all the Socialist
government's doing; 'November traitors' was what they were all
right. And what if someone – this Hitler, say, or someone else like
him – were to make common cause with the army – get Ludendorff
or some of the other war heroes behind him? What then?

'That can't happen, can it?' said Margarete, grasping her
husband's hand. 'Ludendorff *wouldn't*.'

'No, Gretl,' said Benno, 'it can't. He wouldn't.' He patted her hand
reassuringly. 'First of all, look at this Hitler fellow. He's a penni-
less bum, a Viennese tramp, an ex-corporal, for goodness' sake.
An anti-Semite, an ignoramus about economics, a political
neophyte. He'll crash just as quickly as he rises – *if* he rises at
all. And even if Hitler should gain some kind of following among
the riff-raff, do you imagine anyone of General Ludendorff's stature
would ever even *stand* beside such a clownish figure, would even
shake his hand? Make common cause with him? Never.'

'And what's more, Benno,' said Gottfried Büchner, the well-
known film critic, 'don't forget: we still have a society founded
on law and order.'

'And liberty and justice,' said someone else. 'Those principles
are part of the grand German tradition. And now they're encoded
in the new constitution. Liberty and justice are the law of the land.
And our legal system – we have a strong legal system of due
process and courts and judges. If all else fails, our legal system
will protect us against revolution and chaos.'

'I don't think it will,' said a young man sitting beside the piano.
He had a foreign accent. 'I don't think you can count on the
German justice system. That's just my opinion, of course.'
Everyone looked at him. The room went silent. Edvin Lindstrom
was a Swedish consular officer stationed in Munich. It was his
first time at the Horvaths'.

'Explain yourself,' said the essayist. He did not like the idea of
being lectured to about German society by a foreigner.

'Well,' said Edvin, meeting the objection head on, 'as a foreigner stationed here in an official capacity, I may have a better vantage point than you Germans do.' There were a few indignant mutterings around the room, but Edvin forged ahead. 'In my work I come in contact with the justice system at its various levels every day. I see the gears turning, and I see them being greased and manipulated. I watch cases being investigated. I see charges brought or not brought, cases tried or not tried, and in my experience your legal system is . . . unreliable. It has, in the few years since the war ended, become more and more politicized. Cases are decided more and more, not on the merits of a case, but on the *political* merits, on whose ox is being gored . . .'

'*Oh, come on!*' The man sitting next to Willi could restrain himself no longer. As Lindstrom had been speaking, the man's already florid face had gotten redder and redder. His blond mustache bristled. He brushed it furiously with the back of his hand. *Geheimrat* Gerhardt Riegelmann had once been privy counselor to the Bavarian King Ludwig. And though the monarchy was over, at least for the moment, and Riegelmann now headed up an association of mining and smelting interests, he continued to insist proudly on his royal title.

Geheimrat Riegelmann also had regular dealings with the legal system. He was quite certain his finger lay firmly on the pulse of the Bavarian nation. In any case, he knew better than any foreigner ever could how things worked. 'Thankfully,' he said, '*I* do *not* see the German legal system from outside, but rather from inside its beating heart, and on a daily basis. In my considered opinion, you are as wrong as anyone could possibly be.

'*Of course* the legal system is infused with politics. It always has been. How could it be otherwise? It is made up of and operated by people with political convictions. However, I can assure you that we Germans are committed to seeing that the law is administered and carried out fairly and justly. Our officials – from the police all the way up to the attorneys and judges – lay their prejudices aside and bring cases and render judgments in an even-handed way. I assure you, *mein Herr*, justice is blind.'

'Maybe it's a good thing justice is blind,' said Benno. 'She might not like some of the things done in her name if she could see them.'

Several people laughed at the joke, but not *Geheimrat* Riegelmann.

'What do you think, Willi?' said Benno. 'What's your view of the German justice system? Willi is a detective,' he added.

Although Willi might not have agreed with Lindstrom's dire judgment *before* the armory theft and the newspaper bombing, those two events had caused him to begin having his own doubts about the legal system. The armory theft had been short-circuited by the department's chief of detectives to protect the actual thieves, who Willi suspected were army officers and members of a right-wing Freikorps, one of those private armies that were everywhere these days. The two night guards were scapegoats; they had been railroaded into long prison sentences in a rigged trial. And a similar subversion of justice was underway with the newspaper bombing. Willi had begun to wonder to what extent this corruption permeated the larger justice system. The *Geheimrat*'s too vigorous defense of the German justice system did nothing to reassure him. Willi smiled, shrugged, and remained silent.

The *Geheimrat* forged ahead. 'Overseeing justice means protecting society, or perhaps you don't agree?'

Edvin Lindstrom did not answer.

'You may do things differently in Sweden,' said Riegelmann. 'But when our German way of life is under attack, the courts are there to assure that such attacks are unsuccessful. When society is undermined, the courts are there to see that the malefactors are brought to justice.'

'Maybe, whatever we may think of Herr Hitler's ways, we should pay attention to his call for a new *idea* of justice,' said a youngish woman from across the room. 'What's wrong with a justice system that *doesn't* treat those who want to destroy society and us decent, peace-loving citizens as deserving equal protection under the law? Maybe those who want to bring Germany to its knees *should be* punished. Maybe we decent members of society *shouldn't* be punished for defending ourselves against these cultural enemies. Is it wrong to discriminate in the legal system against Bolsheviks and anarchists? I don't think so. What do you think, *Herr Geheimrat*?'

Riegelmann brushed at his mustache and decided that this was a moment for judicious discretion. 'In *my* courtroom,' he said, 'anyone brought before me would always be treated with the utmost fairness. If I were a judge.'

'That is reassuring,' said Willi. He took a sip of his beer and smiled slightly. But he regretted having spoken at all.

At that moment, on the street below, there was the crash of breaking glass, followed by shouts and cries. Willi was on his feet in an instant. 'Everyone stay where you are,' he said. 'And lock the door behind me.' He pulled a revolver from the pocket of his coat hanging by the door and went down the stairs three at a time. He heard someone clattering down the stairs behind him. It was Edvin Lindstrom, the Swede.

A gang of young men in brown shirts and armbands had surrounded a man and a woman on the stoop. Two men held the woman by the arms, while the others took turns punching the man. 'Stop! Police!' shouted Willi as he threw open the door. The men ran off, shouting curses that turned to laughter once they were a safe distance away. Sigrid and Peter Melzer had been on their way to the Horvaths' when they had been chased and accosted by a half-dozen storm troopers.

Willi and Edvin helped the Melzers into the lift and then into the Horvaths' apartment, where everyone stood waiting by the door. Sigrid was more frightened than hurt; Peter was bruised and had a bloody nose. Peter sat at the kitchen table with his head back and a wet washcloth pressed against his nose. When they were able, Willi took statements from them. The other guests waited in silence in the drawing room, thinking about what had just happened but not knowing what to say.

'I think,' said Gerhardt Riegelmann finally, 'this incident confirms my hopeful view of the German justice system, wouldn't you say?' He was speaking to everyone but looking at the Swede. 'The police this evening, in the person of the detective here, restored order, and did so in a laudably quick and efficient manner. At this moment he is interviewing the victims of the crime, gathering information with which he can build a case. I have no doubt the malefactors will be sought, and when they are found, they will be brought to justice. They will inevitably end up punished for their crimes. What do you say to that?'

Edvin Lindstrom had nothing to say, and neither did anyone else.

THE *MUNICH POST*

Maximilian started each day at the *Post* by scanning the wire to see what was going on. Then he set out walking. He drew life as he came upon it – early morning whores around the square, legless veterans, early bread lines, priests at first mass, Nazi rallies, marching storm troopers, picket lines, food markets with empty shelves, street waifs, rich businessmen in their Daimlers and Duesenbergs with fat cigars clenched in their jaws. Maximilian did not make judgments or editorialize in his drawings. He just drew Munich.

One morning there was a letter waiting on his otherwise empty desk. He stared at it for a while. He didn't know anyone who would write him a letter. *Dear Mister Wolf*, it said, *I would like to talk to you about exhibiting your drawings. Please stop by the gallery.* A business card was attached: Aaron Appelbaum, Appelbaum Gallery, Berlin / Munich / London / New York.

Sophie found the letter in his jacket pocket a week later.

'How long have you been carrying this around?' she said.

'Not long,' he said.

'Do you know who this is?' she said.

'I'm not sure I want to show my work,' he said.

'You're not sure,' she said, 'so talk to him. See what he says.'

Aaron Appelbaum was a small, roundish man, with a gentle, soft face and intelligent brown eyes. He took Maximilian's hand in both of his and shook it. 'I greatly admire your work,' he said. He and Maximilian walked around the gallery together looking at the current exhibit – recent small paintings by Otto Dix.

'Your drawings are very strong,' Aaron said. 'Like Dix. But Dix is hard. People don't want to be confronted, you know. And yet he has several collectors. I don't know whether I can sell your work. But I would like to try. They need to be seen in person and not just in the *Münchener Post*. They need to be matted and in frames, on people's walls.'

'I'm not sure I want to sell my work,' said Maximilian.

'Why not?' Aaron said.

'I'm afraid that will ruin it for me. The drawing, I mean.'

'How might that happen?' said Aaron.

'I don't want to feel torn between the drawing and the money.'

'I understand what you're saying. But . . .' Aaron laughed lightly, a sweet, birdlike chortle, '. . . I don't think you need to worry too much about that yet. As I said, these will be a hard sell. So, first of all, we have to get them seen. And you do want them seen, don't you? And really, that's what I want too.'

Aaron offered Maximilian a show in December, which was several months away.

'I can come to your studio and look over your work.'

'I don't have a studio; everything is at the *Post*.'

'I can come to the *Post* then. Or you can bring some drawings – your favorites, and we'll go through them together.'

Maximilian agreed to bring some drawings. 'But I'm still not sure.'

'No,' said Aaron, patting Maximilian's shoulder. 'I know. We'll see.'

Elizabeth Grynbaum installed Sophie in her bed after she came home from the hospital. And Elizabeth moved into Sophie's room. 'I can sleep on a narrow bed,' she said. 'I'm blessed with good sleep wherever I am.'

Between Elizabeth, Maximilian, and Inge, Maximilian's sister – Elizabeth paid her a little – Sophie always had someone at her side. Sophie got out of bed for the first time several months after the bombing. Her first few steps propped up by Inge and Maximilian were tentative. But she did exercises – squatting and then standing, stretching her legs behind her, and lifting her knees against her chest – and little by little her strength came back. She walked in the neighborhood, first to the corner and back, then around the block, then further and further afield.

One Sunday she and Maximilian took the train to Bad Aibling, forty minutes southeast of the city. She had been there once as a child and remembered it as beautiful. They walked on tiny farm roads for two hours, passing wayside crosses, country churches, pastures, fields where the hay had been cut and stacked. They sat in the sun on the terrace of Zum Braumeister, a small *Gasthaus* facing the shimmering snow-covered Alps to their east and drank cold beer with lemonade. Then they walked some more and only stopped because the sun was setting.

One day, a year and half after the bombing, Sophie said, 'I'm going to look for work.'

'Isn't it too soon?' said Maximilian. But Sophie needed to work. And yet Maximilian still tried to put on the brakes. She still had occasional dizzy spells, and sometimes she saw double. 'That will always be with you,' said the doctor. 'It's nerve damage. But you're strong again and working will do you good.'

'The doctor said that?' said Maximilian.

'He did,' said Sophie. She touched his face and kissed him. She was going to work no matter what he or anyone else said.

'Go to the *Post*,' he said. 'See Franz Ortner, the editor. They're expecting you.'

Franz Ortner read through Sophie's clips. He showed them to the city editor. They offered her a job as a reporter. 'I want you to work with Peter Danziger,' Ortner said. Danziger was an ex-boxer, who was now a driver for the paper and also part of their security force. They needed one, thanks to their vivid opposition to fascists of every stripe, including Hitler's party, the NSDAP.

'I know what you're going to say,' said Ortner. 'You want to work alone. But they know who you are. And don't pretend you don't know who I mean. They're not going to let up just because you were injured. They'll double down now that you're at the *Post*.

'So, that's my condition. Follow Kahr, Lossow, Seisser.' (Gustav Ritter von Kahr was the State Commissioner of Bavaria; General Otto von Lossow was the army commander and Hans Ritter von Seisser was the head of the state police. Together the three of them controlled Bavaria.) 'Talk to them, if they'll let you, which I doubt. Talk to the people around them; I can give you names. The situation's fluid and there's all sorts of loose talk. Do what you have to do. But *wherever* you go, *whenever* you go, take Danziger. We're under martial law and the situation is dangerous.'

'I know all that, but . . .'

'No, there's no "but". That's the way it is.'

Peter Danziger had a battered nose, cauliflower ears, and a devilish gap-tooth smile. He took her hand in his gigantic paw. She looked at him warily. He could see what she was thinking. 'Don't worry, honey,' he said with a laugh. 'I'm more attracted to your boyfriend than I am to you.'

THE PUTSCH

Against all odds, Sophie landed an interview with State Commissioner von Kahr. His advisor, Egon Leitner, saw value in his talking to someone from the *Post*.

'That's ridiculous,' said von Kahr. 'It's out of the question. That paper is the enemy. It's a thorn in my side.'

'Which is exactly why you should see her. She was blown up when her old paper's offices were attacked.'

'Which paper?'

'Baron von Plottwietz's *Neue Deutsche Bild*.'

'Oh, yes, I remember. So, she's at the *Post* now, but you're saying she's with us?'

'No, she's *not* with us. But she may be malleable. In any case, she'll listen to what you say. You get to make your best case against Berlin. You've got nothing to lose and a great deal to gain.'

The steps and entrance to the State Chancellery building were guarded by a squad of armed soldiers in battle gear, including a machine-gunner behind a wall of sandbags tucked in at the top of the stairs. After showing their papers, Sophie and Peter Danziger were admitted to the great hall, where they had to show their papers again.

Peter waited on a bench beside the security desk, while Sophie was escorted into the commissioner's office. The office's dark paneled walls were hung with portraits of men – former governors and commissioners, all wearing black suits, some bedecked with ribbons and sashes. High above them was a lavishly decorated plaster ceiling with rosettes and other curlicues. An enormous crystal chandelier hung from a medallion above the commissioner's massive desk and illuminated the portrait of Ludwig III, the former King of Bavaria. The commissioner snapped his heels together and shook hands with Sophie. His mustache was parted by what was meant to be a smile.

After half an hour Sophie emerged from the office and she and Peter left the building.

'How was it?' said Peter.

'He's worse than I thought,' she said, 'all Fatherland and betrayal. Whatever I asked, the answer was the same crap we've heard over and over from them: for the sake of the German people, Versailles must be abrogated. The French must be driven from the Ruhr. Berlin's state of emergency is a violation of Bavarian sovereignty. Blah, blah. They've got plans, he said, but I couldn't get anything out of him. Whatever they're up to will be revealed, he said, at a public meeting November eighth.'

'Did he say anything about bringing back the monarchy, putting the Wittelsbachs back on the Bavarian throne?'

'No, why would he? Where did you get that?'

'They talked about it at the security desk.'

'You asked them?'

'Not exactly.' Peter Danziger had been the Bavarian heavyweight champion not too many years before, which was not much in the boxing world at large but was a big deal in Munich. Everyone remembered the time in Berlin he had knocked Jack Dempsey out of the ring. Of course Dempsey climbed back in and knocked Peter out cold in the next round.

So the men at the desk recognized Peter and, after a little fight talk – which country produced the best fighters, that sort of thing – they meandered off into politics.

Remember how Bavaria had been ruled by the Wittelsbachs? they said. Seven hundred glorious years. Though they were too young to remember, they talked about it as though it were yesterday. And wouldn't it be great to bring back the king? To hell with the Prussians and their Reich. How about the Kingdom of Bavaria? 'It's going to happen,' said the guard sitting next to Peter.

'Nah, that'll never happen,' said Peter.

The guard leaned in closer. 'Prince Rupprecht has been to see the commissioner,' he whispered.

'So what?' said Peter.

'At least three times in the last week,' said the guard. 'Oh, it's going to happen all right.' Rupprecht was the son of Ludwig III, the last King of Bavaria.

A NEW BAVARIAN KINGDOM? was the headline over the front-page story, by Sophie Auerbach and Peter Danziger. It was Peter's first byline. 'Where in the hell did they get this?' von Kahr wanted to know. He was furious. Egon Leitner swore he didn't know. 'Did

she talk to that Hitler asshole?' said Kahr. 'That lunatic keeps
hounding me about the Wittelsbachs.'

'I doubt that he'd ever talk to the *Post* about anything, much
less about the Wittelsbachs. Restoration's the last thing he wants.
And the prince thinks Hitler's insane. Anyway, maybe it's not such
a bad thing, the article. I mean, you want a big turnout on the
eighth, don't you? Well, stories like this are just the thing to get
people to show up.'

Egon Leitner was right. The evening of the eighth, Sophie, Peter,
and Maximilian made their way through crowds milling and
jostling outside the Bürgerbräukeller despite the sleet and rain. If
you wanted to hold a large public meeting in Munich, a beer hall
was the place to do it. And the largest, like the Bürgerbräukeller,
could seat thousands. That it could provide beer was an added
benefit. The gigantic hall was packed.

Kahr rose a little after eight and started speaking. He spoke yet
again about the inflation and the general mismanagement of the
economy by the Socialist government in Berlin, whose answer to
everything seemed to be to declare a national emergency and
to print more money. 'Has that solved anything? *Will* it solve
anything?' There were hoots of derision from the crowd. 'You're
right. The solution lies in *our* hands.'

Suddenly there was a commotion in the back of the room. Kahr
craned his neck. Von Lossow and von Seisser stood up beside him
to see what was going on. Adolf Hitler, who had appeared out of
nowhere, climbed onto a table and fired a pistol into the ceiling.
Having everyone's attention, he jumped down and, surrounded by
storm troopers in brown shirts, pushed his way forward. He stuck
his pistol in the face of a policeman who tried to stop him. He
climbed onstage, pushed Kahr aside, and seized the microphone.

The next day, the *Munich Post* had an editorial at the top of
page one.

A DANGEROUS FARCE

Yesterday evening at the Bürgerbräukeller, Adolf Hitler,
the delusional Austrian corporal and failed artist who
fancies himself the savior of Germany, tried to stage a
coup. He seized the microphone from Gustav von Kahr and

*proclaimed 'the national revolution'. He said the governments
in Berlin and Bavaria had been removed, and a provisional
national government had been formed. He said the army and
the police were marching under the Swastika flag.*

*Everything Adolf Hitler said was an outright lie. The
governments in Munich and Berlin were and are intact and
no provisional government has been formed. Hitler announced,
furthermore, that General Ludendorff, the tottering and now
tarnished war hero, would take over the new German army
and together they would march on Berlin and take over the
reins of power. Hitler's revolution is founded on lies and
violence, and, except in his own deranged mind and in the
minds of his deluded rabble, it does not exist at all.*

*The evening's events and the events that followed might
be described as a raucous farce, did they not come at such a
dangerous moment in our nation's history and do such
momentous injury to our democracy. Do not think that because
Hitler is insane and his ideas are crackpot they cannot come
into being. If we the German people sit back and do nothing,
if we tolerate this disgusting criminal and his violent and
unconstitutional behavior, then we will be as guilty as Adolf
Hitler himself when his crimes are reckoned.*

There followed a number of other stories about the evening's events
along with a series of drawings by Maximilian, including one of a
wild-eyed Hitler pointing his pistol at a policeman.

KONRAD MILCH

K onrad Milch was the ninth and last child of Hermann Milch, a farmer in a Bavarian village not far from Salzburg, and his third wife, Nina. Gertrude, Hermann's first wife, had married him when they were both thirty. Why she did was anybody's guess. He was a cold and brutal man, incapable of giving or receiving tenderness. When he was overcome by lust, he tore Gertrude's clothes off and poked and jabbed at her until he ejaculated. She died when she was forty, many said from being married to Hermann. They had no children.

Angele, Hermann's second wife, died in childbirth the year after they married, along with their only child. Next Hermann married Nina, a nineteen-year-old girl of limited intelligence, when he was fifty, and only then because he had made her pregnant.

Hermann had learned nothing from his first two marriages, unless it was new variations of cruelty. Nina got pregnant nearly every time Hermann assaulted her. But she saw these pregnancies as advantageous. Once she was pregnant, Hermann left her alone. She gave birth to nine healthy children in rapid order. She was a loving but incapable mother. She couldn't take care of herself, let alone nine children. And Hermann was as indifferent to his own children as he was to the hog he killed every New Year's Day. Nina and the children lived in violence and squalor.

Irena, the eldest of the Milch children, was the one bright light in this dark household. She was intelligent and sweet and dedicated to her siblings and, most amazingly, to her parents. Her father abused her no less than he abused everyone else, but Irena believed that kindness could heal whatever misery caused his brutality. In return for his hateful treatment, she was unfailingly kind.

Irena was thirteen when Konrad was born. By then she had been a surrogate mother to her siblings nearly as long as she could remember. She was kind and fiercely protective of them, even to the point of defying her father, which only incited further rage and cruelty.

By the time Konrad was fifteen, he and Irena were the last of

Hermann's children still living under his roof. As the other children had left home, Irena had devoted herself more and more to protecting Konrad. And as her devotion to Konrad increased, Hermann's hatred of the boy grew. Hermann mocked and belittled Konrad constantly. Irena had gotten used to Hermann's bad treatment, but Konrad never did.

Konrad's one refuge was singing. He had a beautiful tenor voice and could lose himself in a song. But when Konrad sang Hermann flew into a rage and attacked him. Hermann had never known beauty or happiness, so to see or hear it in others, especially his own son, was like witnessing a disloyal act, treachery of the worst kind. Konrad did the only thing he could in order to survive: he stopped singing. After that, there was nothing he loved in the world, except Irena.

The morning had dawned beautifully. Hermann was heating his coffee on the kitchen fire. Konrad was in the barn feeding the pigs. Without thinking, he started singing. You could barely hear it in the house, like the faint warbling of a distant bird. But Hermann tore out of the house and into the barn. 'I told you I don't want to hear that shit!' he said. He picked up a broken ax handle and swung it at Konrad. Konrad grabbed the handle and tore it from Hermann's hand. When had the little bastard gotten so big and strong? Hermann wondered, just as the ax handle caught him across the head and knocked him in among the pigs. They squealed and ran every which way, including across Hermann lying dazed in the mud.

That moment Konrad decided to leave. Irena begged him not to go. 'You'll be all right here, Irena,' he said. 'But if I stay, next time I'll kill him. I've got to go.'

He got to Munich in the first spring after the war and soon fell in with a gang of black-marketeers, stealing and running errands for them at first, and then eventually working as hired muscle. He was still only sixteen, but he was big and strong and quick to fight.

Konrad didn't care about politics. It was all crap, as far as he was concerned. But he understood feeling powerless. It filled him with rage. The National Socialist Workers, or whatever they called themselves, wanted to give power back to the embittered and the angry, and that spoke to Konrad.

The Party wanted enforcers – they called them the Sturmabteilung, the SA, the storm troopers; Konrad liked the sound of *that* – to keep order at their meetings, to break Communist, Socialist, Jew, you-name-it, skulls. They broke up opposition meetings and rallies, or beat up members of rival organizations, or whatever was called for. Konrad quickly acquired a reputation for toughness and a hair trigger. Anything could set him off, and he was fearless. He waded in, fists swinging. He had become his father's son.

Konrad's first big job was rolling that grenade into the newspaper office and blowing those shitheads to smithereens. The guy with him that day – Otto; he didn't know his last name – was older and had been to university. Studied theology or something. He had lost a hand in the war. But he was too cautious. Scared really. Konrad didn't like him.

Konrad was at the Bürgerbräukeller that night. He was part of the group that had gotten Hitler to the front of the room when he took over the meeting. Konrad had knocked a cop right on his fat ass. The next morning, still at the beer hall and frustrated by their efforts to enlist Kahr and the other Bavarian officials in their enterprise, Hitler and General Ludendorff put together an army of two thousand storm troopers and other supporters and set out for the city once more. This time they were armed with rifles and bayonets and intended to take over the War Ministry. Once they controlled the War Ministry, they would control the army. And with the army they could march to Berlin and bring down the entire national government. It was a coup d'état.

As they marched toward the city, they were stopped by police at the Ludwigsbrücke, the bridge over the Isar River. But when they threatened to kill members of the city council they had taken hostage the night before, the police stood aside and let them pass. Konrad sneered at the cops and shouted obscenities as the column marched past. And when his comrades started singing 'The Rotten Bones are Trembling', his heart soared. This, he thought, is where I belong.

Wir werden weiter marschieren
Wenn alles in Scherben fällt,
Denn heute gehört uns Deutschland
Und morgen die ganze Welt.
(We will march on, when everything falls to bits. Because today Germany belongs to us, and tomorrow the whole world.)

As soon as word reached the *Post* that Ludendorff, Hitler, and their army of storm troopers were on the move, Sophie and Peter set out for the War Ministry. At that moment the column of men was passing through the Isar Gate and entering the old city. They were almost certainly headed toward Ludwigstraße. The army was on high alert and posted around the War Ministry, along Ludwigstraße, at the Odeonsplatz, and with a large contingent at the Feldherrnhalle – the war memorial – where Ludwigstraße divided into narrow passages on either side of the building. Machine guns had been set up. The infantry waited with fixed bayonets.

Maximilian headed toward the marchers. He heard them coming before he saw them. Their marching feet and their shouts and singing echoed through the narrow streets of the old city. They were bedraggled, some in uniforms, most not. But they were armed and followed by trucks full of armed men. They carried Swastika flags and banners. Hitler, in his shabby trenchcoat and fedora, General Ludendorff, in his dress uniform, and Hermann Göring were in the lead.

Maximilian made quick sketches, turning the pages of his notebook as soon as he had drawn a few key lines. He would finish the drawings later. He caught Hitler – skinny and haunted – and Göring, the famous fighter ace. Ludendorff looked like he didn't quite know where he was. He had meant to make history, but it had all gotten away from him.

Maximilian had never seen Konrad Milch before. He had no idea who he was. And it had been two years now since, with Walther Hinzig's help, he had drawn his portrait. But, because he had drawn him over and over back then, Konrad's face, with its narrow eyes, heavy brow, turned-up nose, the mouth without lips, the cleft chin, was burned into his memory. He found himself drawing it again, as he passed not ten meters in front of him. It took him a moment to realize why the face was familiar. And as Maximilian looked and drew, looked again and drew, Konrad stared back.

Konrad didn't know Maximilian, of course. He obviously had no idea of their connection. But he knew this guy was drawing his picture and he didn't like it. Just as Maximilian looked up from drawing, Konrad's fist slammed into his chest, knocking him against a lamppost. The next punch knocked him to the ground.

'Come on, Konrad.' Two of Konrad's SA comrades pulled him back into the march as Maximilian struggled to his feet. Konrad rejoined the march, looking back at Maximilian all the while, aiming his balled fist at him. 'I'll get you, asshole,' he said, mouthing the words.

The main contingent of storm troopers that had besieged the

War Ministry early that morning was still blocked and completely surrounded by the army. Men on both sides had fought side by side not many years before. They were brothers in arms. They had no appetite for fighting each other. Before long, though, everyone heard the thunder of marching feet as the column led by Hitler and General Ludendorff turned up the narrow Residenzstraße. A light wet snow was falling again. A detachment of police waited with carbines and pistols at the ready. As Hitler and his motley army approached the Feldherrnhalle the police raised their weapons. The marchers at the front of the column stopped twenty meters from the police line, while the rear of the column pressed forward filling the street.

'Surrender!' shouted Hitler to the police. 'Surrender to the German people!'

'General Ludendorff is here!' shouted someone else. 'Surrender!'

Then the square went quiet.

A police captain mounted the stairs of the Feldherrnhalle and, standing between the great stone lions and speaking through a megaphone, said, 'You are in violation of city ordinances and laws of the German Reich. You are hereby ordered to disperse or face arrest.'

'It is *you* who are in violation of the law,' shouted someone. Was it Hitler? Sophie couldn't tell from her vantage point behind the column of marchers. There were angry shouts from the storm troopers behind Hitler.

'We shit on the Republic!'

'Join us or get out of the way!'

'We are the Reich.' Then someone fired a shot, and in an instant there was gunfire from every direction. For a minute the air was full of bullets, whizzing about like angry hornets, ricocheting this way and that. Sophie squeezed further into the doorway where she stood. Then everything went quiet.

Men were on the ground across the square. Hitler was down but he wasn't hit; Göring was shot in the hip. Hitler scuttled along the pavement like a crab, ran into a side street, jumped into a waiting car, and was driven away. Others who could jumped up and ran. Ludendorff had remained standing. And now he resumed marching and passed unmolested through the line of police. He was placed under arrest. Fourteen storm troopers and four police were dead or dying, and many others lay wounded and groaning on the square.

THE ARTIST

When Willi Geismeier came into the station the next morning, the desk sergeant said, 'There's someone waiting to see you.'

'Who?'

'Maximilian Wolf.'

'What's it about?' said Willi.

'He wouldn't say.'

Willi backed up a few steps to the window to the waiting room and, after a moment, recognized Maximilian. It had been how long – two years? – since they had seen each other. He went out to him.

Maximilian rose and held out his hand. 'Herr Geismeier, I'm Maximilian Wolf.'

'Yes, I remember you, Herr Wolf,' said Willi. 'I see your drawings in the *Post*. How are you?' He gestured in the direction of Maximilian's face. 'What happened to you?'

Maximilian had a large purple bruise under his right eye, and the eye was severely bloodshot.

'Well,' said Maximilian, 'actually, it has to do with why I'm here. I haven't heard from you about the bombing since it happened. I'm guessing that means there are no new developments and you're no closer to knowing who did it.'

'They took me off the case, Herr Wolf, so I'm not working on it any longer. Detective Sergeant Gruber is in charge of it, if you need to talk to someone.' Willi was mostly on desk duty these days or working home break-ins, store robberies, that sort of thing. 'How is Fräulein . . .' He couldn't remember her name.

'Auerbach. Sophie Auerbach,' said Maximilian. 'She's doing well. She's mostly recovered from her injuries.'

'I'm glad to hear that. Look, I'm sorry no one has been in touch, Herr Wolf. Someone should have been. But, frankly, the case had gone cold, even while I was still on it. And now it's been almost two years, if I remember correctly. I still show the drawings around, when it's . . . appropriate. Neither one of the men you drew is in our files as far as anyone can tell. And other than your drawings, there was nothing to go on. As far as I can tell, there still isn't.'

'Does Detective Gruber have the drawings?' said Maximilian. 'I remember, you weren't going to show them to him.'

'No, that's right. I never did. And . . . I don't want to.'

'I think I understand,' said Maximilian. 'Can we go somewhere more private?' People were passing nearby. 'I want to show you something.'

They went into an interview room. Willi closed the door. Maximilian took that day's *Post* from his pocket and handed it to Willi.

'I don't have a lot of time,' said Willi. 'What with yesterday's events and all. What am I looking for here?'

'Look at the drawings on page two.'

Willi opened the paper and looked. Then he recognized the drawing of Konrad and looked again. 'Where was this?' he said. 'Is this from the march?'

'The Putsch, yeah. Just below Residenzstraße and the Feldherrnhalle.'

'So he was there.'

'Marching with the brownshirts.'

'Did he see you?'

Maximilian pointed at the bruise. 'Yeah. He did this. He didn't like me drawing him. He doesn't know who I am, or that I have any connection to the bombing. He just didn't like being drawn.'

'Maybe,' said Willi. 'Except you drew for the *Bild* and now draw for the *Post*, so, unless he's an idiot, it won't be too hard for him to make the connection and find you.' Willi looked at Maximilian without speaking. Then his eyes darted around the room in that odd way he had when he was thinking. He walked to the end of the room, turned around and walked back.

'You recognize that you've put yourself into a . . . situation, Herr Wolf? I mean, first of all, you've inserted yourself right in the middle of an ongoing police investigation. *And* you've put yourself in danger.'

'*Is* there an ongoing police investigation, Herr Geismeier? You said yourself you've reached a dead end. As far as I can see nothing is going on.'

'I wouldn't call it a dead end. I'd call it stalled. In any case, that doesn't concern you.'

'Well, now I've brought you this.' He tapped the newspaper with the back of his hand. 'That could be the very thing to get the investigation going again, couldn't it?'

'I wish you had just brought it to me instead of . . . this.' Willi took the paper from Maximilian and looked at it again. 'This guy – we don't even know his name – now knows all about you: who you are, where you work, and that you're interested in him.'

'Konrad,' said Maximilian.

'What?'

'His name is Konrad. The guys that pulled him off me called him Konrad. I don't know his last name.'

'Well, that's just great. So, what did you think you were doing putting this in the paper? Why didn't you just bring it to me?'

'And what would you have done with it that you couldn't do with the first drawing?'

'Knowing more about who he is, where he has been, who he's connected to, we could have resumed our search for Konrad and probably found him. So,' said Willi, 'why put it in the paper?'

'So that he'll come looking for me,' said Maximilian.

'Probably he won't just smack you in the face next time. If he didn't like you drawing him he's not going to like you putting your drawing in the paper, that's for sure. This guy's a killer, Herr Wolf, and you just hung a big fat bullseye on your back.'

THE DETECTIVE SERGEANT

With Hermann Gruber's promotion to detective sergeant, the dynamics in the squad changed. A reorganization had been ordered from the top, with Gruber put in charge of the squad which up to now had been under Captain Reineke's direct supervision. Reineke, who was seen by higher ups as 'reliable', that is favorable to the NSDAP, had also been promoted, and now oversaw multiple detective squads. The reorganized squad under Gruber included seven detectives, four of whom – including Gruber – were also NSDAP storm troopers. Willi did not have a partner and had been shunted onto make-work cases, which Reineke thought would keep him busy and diminish the possibility that he might get up to mischief.

During his brief tenure as a detective, Gruber's main purpose had been advancing his own career, which he had done by concealing the willful incompetence and growing malfeasance of police higher-ups favorable to Hitler. Gruber had only ever investigated a crime in order to discover how to cover it up. For Willi, being without a partner and dealing with make-work meant to him that he could investigate crimes as he saw fit. As long as he kept his closure rate high – which he did by solving petty crimes and misdemeanors – nobody seemed to bother him, and he could continue to investigate crimes he had been ordered to stay away from. Which he did.

Willi knocked on Gruber's office door. 'Come in, Geismeier,' said Hermann. 'What is it?' Hermann took his cues from his mentor Captain Reineke, and, with his promotion, had taken on all the officiousness and pomp that he imagined went with the position of detective sergeant. He wore the brown uniform with his pants tucked into polished knee-high boots. His brown tie was snugged up as tight as it would go and hung squarely across his thickening belly. The overcoat, belts, holster, and pistol hung nearby. The sight of Willi's shirttail half out and tie poorly knotted caused Hermann to scowl. 'What do you want, Geismeier?'

'Have you seen this, Sergeant?' said Willi, handing Hermann the *Post*.

'The *Munich Pest*.' Gruber laughed at his own cleverness. 'Of course not, Geismeier. Nobody reads the goddamn *Pest*.'

'We should know our enemy, don't you think, sir?'

'What is it you want me to look at?'

'Page two. The pictures.' Willi watched Hermann's eyes as they scanned down the page and lingered a moment too long on Konrad Milch.

'What about them?' said Hermann.

'I'm looking into an assault complaint,' said Willi. 'That guy in the picture. He fits the description of the assailant in a mugging.'

'Which guy?' said Hermann, although, besides Hitler and Göring, there was only one individual depicted.

'That one.' Willi leaned over and tapped the picture. 'There's probably nothing to it, but . . .'

'If you think there's nothing to it, then why are you looking into it?'

'Leaving no stone unturned, Sergeant. Crossing the t's and dotting the i's.'

'OK, OK. Keep looking, Geismeier. And if you find anything, be sure to let me know. But for heaven's sake, don't waste department time on vague leads like this.'

'Yes, sir,' said Willi.

'What else are you working on right now?' said Gruber, realizing suddenly he had no idea what Willi was up to. Willi started listing cases by name and then going into too much detail. Gruber cut him off. 'OK, fine, fine,' he said. 'Just keep me up to date, Geismeier.'

'Yes, sir.'

'Is there anything else?'

'No, sir,' said Willi.

'Dismissed,' said Detective Sergeant Gruber, but by then he was talking to Willi's back.

HONORING THE DEAD

The ruling Bavarian triumvirate had been duped and nearly unseated by Hitler's revolt. One shot fired into the ceiling of a beer hall and a series of brazen and, in retrospect, transparent lies had been sufficient to bamboozle the Bavarian State Commissioner, the commanding general of the Reichswehr in Bavaria, and the head of the State Police into joining forces with someone who, on reflection, they could all agree was deranged. They had to do something to regain their authority and the respect of the Bavarian people.

Consequently, State Commissioner von Kahr issued a proclamation that was published in all the newspapers and posted on kiosks all over the city. He condemned in the strongest terms the deceit of the triumvirate by 'ambitious comrades' – meaning Hitler and Ludendorff – which had resulted in disorder, lawlessness, and 'a scene of disgusting violence.'

To consolidate the triumvirate's power among the people, but particularly among the police and the army, von Kahr announced a day of mourning and a grand public ceremony on Odeon Square to honor the fallen heroes. Photos of the four dead policemen stood by the stairs of the Feldherrnhalle on easels draped in black bunting. Large black wreaths with ribbons of blue and white, the Bavarian colors, leaned against the easels. In a show of solidarity, high state and police officials stood in rows beside and behind the podium. Behind them was a full military band.

A cavalry detachment in full parade regalia rode onto the square and stationed themselves around the perimeter. Steam poured from the horses' nostrils; the crash of their iron shoes echoed across the square. The horses stamped their feet and shook and nodded their heads causing the ostrich plumes both they and their riders wore to be tossed this way and that.

A thousand Reichswehr troops marched onto the square in columns of four. They were followed by policemen, also in columns of four. Behind the ranks of police and army stood more city officials and members of the public.

Wearing mourning dress, Gustav Ritter von Kahr stepped to the podium. He spoke about the need for law and order in these difficult and trying times of inflation and poverty and an imminent Bolshevik threat. There was, he said, plenty to object to about the Socialist regime in Berlin. They were allowing the French to run roughshod in the Ruhr and to abuse the German nation. They were making common cause with the Bolsheviks. Changes had to be made. But they had to be made in an orderly and lawful fashion and by the powers that be. 'We are under martial law,' he reminded the crowd, 'which means that political changes will come about only as the ruling Bavarian triumvirate determines that such changes are good for the Bavarian State.'

Colonel Hans Ritter von Seisser, the head of the State Police, spoke next. He told the crowd that the organizers of the riot who were responsible for the loss of life had been caught and were in prison awaiting trial. There were good people on both sides, he said, and he and his colleagues – he gestured toward von Kahr and von Lossow – promised that political differences would never disturb the peace again. The Bavarian State was secure and would remain secure as long as he drew breath.

Willi felt uncomfortable walking home. He mistrusted all ceremony, and the more pomp there was the more he mistrusted it. Willi hadn't worn his uniform in over a year. He was unaccustomed to the feel of the boots, the tight pants, heavy coat and high collar, all the leather belts, the tall leather hat with the chinstrap. He caught a glimpse of his reflection in a shop window and it stopped him short. Willi took off the hat and held it under his arm. He pretended to be looking at the watches displayed in the shop window. A uniform – police, army, it doesn't matter – is a kind of disguise. Whoever you might think you are disappears under the uniform. You become the authority your uniform represents. You are loved, hated, admired, feared, not because of anything about you but because of the uniform you wear.

Willi looked up and saw a man inside the shop watching him. The man looked down and busied himself with something on the counter. Willi looked at the sign on the window: ROSENSTERN – SCHMUCK UND UHREN.

Willi opened the door which rang a bell inside. 'May I help the gentleman?' said the man at the counter.

'Are you the proprietor?' said Willi.

'Yes, sir,' said the man, avoiding Willi's eyes.

'Herr Rosenstern?' said Willi.

'Yes, sir,' said the man, shifting uneasily.

'I'm interested in buying a new watch,' said Willi.

'Does the gentleman have anything in particular in mind?' Franz Rosenstern said.

'Something modern, easy to read,' said Willi. He didn't really know how to shop for watches.

Rosenstern started lining up watches on the counter for Willi to see and compare. 'These are all German watches,' he said. 'This one is made right here in Munich.' He held the watch toward Willi.

'I've heard the Americans make good watches,' said Willi. 'Do you have any American watches?'

Was this a trick question? 'I have some, yes. But German watches are far superior.' Franz Rosenstern was afraid. And why wouldn't he be? The week before, his shop window had been painted with a swastika and the word 'Jude' by a band of young men, while two policemen, wearing the same uniform Willi now wore, watched from across the street. Every question Willi posed, every word he spoke seemed a threat in Franz Rosenstern's eyes. And there was nothing Willi could say that would make it otherwise.

'Thank you for your time, Herr Rosenstern. I can see these are fine watches. I will think about it.'

'I assure you, sir, that my prices are fair and as low as you will find,' said Franz. 'Please, sir . . .' he said, but he didn't finish the sentence. The bell rang as Willi opened the door and left.

It being Saturday, precinct headquarters was empty except for the duty officer. Willi went to his locker, took off the uniform, and put on the clothes he kept there – battered shoes, pants that needed pressing, a shirt, jacket, and a plaid tie. He tried without success to scrape a small stain – it looked like mustard – from the tie. He hung the uniform in the locker and vowed to himself not to wear it again.

THE SHOW

The Appelbaum Gallery was a large, well-lit space on the second floor overlooking the English Garden to the north. It was two days before the *vernissage* for Maximilian's exhibition. Aaron Appelbaum had come back from Berlin to oversee the installation of Maximilian's first show. Thirty of Maximilian's drawings, selected by Maximilian and Aaron, and now matted and framed, were leaning against the gleaming white walls ready to be hung. Two gallery assistants had suspended hanger cables from the wooden railing near the ceiling and were waiting for instructions from Aaron.

Aaron had placed the drawings in the order he wanted them. He had a practiced eye and put drawings side by side so they would complement and enhance one another, sometimes stylistically, sometimes thematically. That was how a drawing of a young couple on a park bench ended up beside a drawing of two soldiers with their heads together looking along the barrel of a machine gun. Aaron walked around the room one last time, occasionally telling an assistant to move this drawing or to reverse those two, wanting to get the arrangement just right. 'All right,' he said after a while. 'Let's start hanging.'

Because of his newspaper work, Maximilian had become known in Munich. And, this being his first show, Aaron was hopeful that the opening would attract a large and enthusiastic crowd. Just to be sure, he had had posters put up on kiosks and advertising columns around the city. He had bought space in the arts pages in various newspapers.

By six o'clock, Friday, though, Aaron was pacing nervously, making certain there was enough wine, enough glasses, that the drawings were all where they should be, that the labels were correct, and worrying that no one would show up. It had been snowing steadily for the whole day, and the forecast was for more snow. He walked around nudging a drawing here and there. But there was really nothing more to be done.

He needn't have worried. By the time Maximilian and Sophie

arrived fifteen minutes early, as they had promised, there were already quite a few people circling through the gallery looking at drawings, leaning in, then stepping back, murmuring to one another.

'These are really quite wonderful, Herr Wolf,' said a tall, elderly man with white hair and a white mustache. His wife nodded in agreement. 'The newspaper doesn't do them justice.' The man then went to Aaron, who spoke to one of the assistants who scurried over and stuck a red dot by a drawing to indicate that it had been sold.

By six, visitors were pouring in, and by six-thirty the room was full of people looking at the drawings and talking animatedly about what they were seeing. A steady stream congratulated Aaron on this wonderful show and Maximilian on his outstanding work. Maximilian was surprised to see the detective Willi Geismeier across the room. Willi was standing not far from the portrait of Konrad. Willi gave Maximilian a faint smile and a nod and then disappeared from view as the crowd closed in front of him.

At nine o'clock, when the event was supposed to end, the room was still full of people. Finally, at ten-thirty people were mostly gone. The gallery assistants showed the last of them out. There were red dots everywhere; most of the drawings had been sold.

Aaron Appelbaum pronounced the show a great success. 'It's a remarkable result for a first show,' he said. Several influential art writers had come, as well as curators from museums in Munich, Cologne, and Berlin. 'A wonderful success,' said Aaron again. 'Well deserved. I think we should think about a show in Berlin.' He shook hands with Maximilian and they raised wine glasses to one another. 'Congratulations,' said Aaron.

The weather forecast had been wrong. The snow had stopped and it had gotten colder. The streetlights had haloes around them. Maximilian wrapped his scarf tighter and pulled his overcoat close around his neck. The fresh snow glistened in the moonlight. Tristanstraße was a fifteen-minute walk, ten if you walked through the English Garden. Sophie took his arm. The snow crunched under their feet as they turned into the park.

The three men were on them in an instant, two grabbing Sophie and tearing her away from Maximilian. The third, Konrad Milch, went at Maximilian, swinging a long piece of metal pipe. He swung at his head but Maximilian slipped sideways and the pipe glanced off his shoulder, knocking him to the ground.

'You're dead, you goddamn Bolshevik!' Konrad screamed and swung again. This time the blow stunned Maximilian. Konrad raised the pipe over his head.

There was a gunshot and Konrad had a surprised look on his face. Maximilian knew that look; he had seen it again and again in the war. Konrad dropped the pipe into the snow, where it sank from sight. He stared at Maximilian, his eyes and his mouth wide open.

Konrad fought to remain standing then took a step. Maybe he thought *acting* normal would mean things *were* normal. But even as he tried to stay upright, his legs gave way and he sank to his knees.

Konrad toppled over face down in the snow. The two other men had vanished. Sophie had broken free. She held a Luger in front of her, the barrel smoking, the smell of gunpowder in the cold night air. Konrad lay at their feet.

Maximilian turned Konrad over. The snow under him had turned pink. He was still alive. His eyes were blinking slowly and his mouth was opening and closing, trying to form words but managing only to form a large pink bubble. His hands jerked about, his feet too.

He tried again to speak. 'Irena,' he whispered. Then again, 'Oh, Irena. Irena. Please.'

'We'll get help,' said Maximilian, not knowing what else to do. Then Konrad stopped moving. He was dead.

BLOOD IN THE SNOW

Willi had gone to the art gallery thinking that Maximilian's exhibition might be too much for Konrad to resist after his portrait was in the paper. Sure enough, two men came into the show around eight-thirty and circled the room until they came to Konrad's portrait. They looked at the drawing, looked at each other, and left. They went to a cafe across the street, where Konrad was waiting.

The cafe was crowded, and the men took no notice as Willi came in and sat across the room with his back to them. He ordered goulash soup and a beer. He read the paper while he ate. The soup was good. The cafe was all but empty when one of the men finally said, 'There he is.' The three men got up and went out. Willi paid his bill and followed them. He took out his gun as he entered the park. The two men ran past him as a shot rang out.

Maximilian was holding Sophie. Konrad lay on the ground. Blood was spreading in the snow under him. 'Are you all right?' said Willi. They were.

'Give me the gun,' said Willi. 'How long have you had it?'

'Since the bombing,' said Maximilian.

'Do you have a permit?' said Willi.

'Yes,' said Sophie. 'Are you arresting me?'

'It was self-defense,' said Maximilian.

Department protocol required, of course, that Willi detain Sophie and Maximilian, call in the shooting, and then wait until uniformed police arrived. If Willi did what he was required to do, Sophie would be held and questioned. Maximilian would be questioned. And he, Willi, would be questioned. Evidence would be gathered. Testimony would be taken.

In the not very distant past, Konrad's friends would have been found, their malevolent intentions would have been discovered, and Sophie would have been judged correctly to have acted in self-defense. But what would happen now?

Now, Willi was fairly certain, Konrad's friends would swear that *they* had been attacked, and, depending on which judge took the case, would be, if not exactly believed, then taken to be plausible and useful. Konrad had tried to defend himself, they'd say. And Sophie had shot him down in cold blood. Here was a chance to lock Sophie and Maximilian, who were demonstrably enemies of Germany, away for a long stretch.

That story was of course preposterous. But it didn't matter anymore. The fourteen Nazis who had died during the Putsch attempt had been lionized in the nationalist press. The Nazis built their movement on martyrs, and Willi was quite certain they would never allow such perfect villains as Sophie and Maximilian – they worked for the *Munich Post* after all – to go unpunished, and such a martyr as Konrad Milch to go uncelebrated. In fact, within days Konrad was being celebrated in the *Völkischer Beobachter*, the Nazi paper, and then in a speech by Hitler himself as 'a German hero and a patriot'.

'Take her home,' said Willi. 'Don't talk to anyone about any of this. Especially the police. As far as they're concerned you went from the gallery straight home. You did not walk through the park.' Willi called in the shooting anonymously from a public phone box at the edge of the English Garden.

That night Willi tossed and turned and finally fell into a restless sleep just before dawn. For the first time in a long time, he dreamed of the trenches. He saw Sophie and Maximilian going over the top, but when he tried to call to them not a sound came out of his mouth. He woke up bathed in sweat. 'I've crossed over,' he said to himself. 'I'm on the wrong side of the law.'

Detective Sergeant Gruber brought up the Milch shooting at the Monday morning briefing. 'Captain says we're to give this the highest priority. This attack was in the English Garden, Friday about midnight. The victim was shot once in the back. The victim has been identified as Konrad Milch.'

'What do we know about him, Sergeant?'

'He was a brave young patriot,' said Gruber.

The detectives and uniformed cops wrote down the name. 'Was it robbery?' someone said.

'It doesn't seem like it,' said Gruber. 'There was money in his billfold, which was still in his pocket. We do know from the tracks in the snow that at least three other people were there. There's evidence of a struggle.' Gruber made no mention of the metal pipe or the pistol that had been found in Milch's pocket.

'But, Sergeant, the English Garden's in the Sixth Precinct,' somebody said. 'Why's this even our case?' The Tenth was short-handed and overloaded with cases.

'I told you,' said Gruber, 'this comes from the captain.'

'Why the high priority?'

'Because the captain says it's high priority,' said Gruber. 'So let's focus: we've had two similar shootings in the Tenth, neither one fatal. But same caliber handgun as Friday night: a 7.65. Maybe a Luger.'

'Who identified the victim?' said Willi.

Gruber looked at his briefing sheet. 'Fedor Blaskowitz.'

'And is this Fedor Blaskowitz a relative?' Willi asked.

'No,' said Gruber after studying the sheet. 'An associate. Anyway, Geismeier, I've put Bergemann and Wendt on the case. We need to catch these killers in a hurry so I'll be briefing them on the details.' Bergemann and Wendt had sympathetic feelings toward Hitler and the NSDAP. And they were lazy.

'Sergeant,' said Willi, 'you want this case closed quickly, am I right?'

'Didn't I just say so, Geismeier?' said Gruber. 'Damn it, man, leave it to Bergemann and Wendt. You have a pile of cases on your desk. Let's see you close some of those.'

Still Willi didn't let up. 'Sir, are you thinking the Milch fellow was assassinated?'

Reineke had already instructed Gruber: when they caught the killer, assassination was to be the charge. How did Geismeier even know that? Or was he just guessing? 'Damn it, Geismeier, what is it with you? Will you quit meddling and mind your own business? For the last time: Bergemann and Wendt are on the case. And they'll follow the evidence where it leads.'

Gruber was worried. His task was to solve the case in a satisfactory fashion making Milch the victim and suppressing the fact that police officials had sanctioned his past crimes. If any of that got out, Gruber's ass was in a sling. The shit always flowed downhill. The *Post* would get hold of it. Other papers too. A genuine catastrophe would ensue.

'Listen, Gruber,' Reineke said that afternoon, 'I'm getting more and more pressure. Geismeier keeps sticking his nose where it doesn't belong.'

'Believe me, Captain, I know,' said Gruber.

'You know, Sergeant? Well, goddamn it, why don't you put a stop to it? Rein him in or better yet, get rid of the son of a bitch.'

'We could fire him, sir. I thought of that. But what would we gain by that?'

'He'd be out of our hair, Gruber. That's what.'

'Yes, he would, Captain. But . . .'

'But?'

'Well, knowing Geismeier, that won't stop him. Besides, if we get rid of him, we'd be throwing away a valuable resource.'

'What do you mean by that, Sergeant? What possible value can you see in that pissant?'

'I agree, sir. Geismeier's a serious problem. But that's because he's a good investigator. So, I'm thinking, why not let him run on a long leash? As long he does, we know where he is and what he's up to. He's like an encyclopedia, Captain. And some of what he knows could be useful. For instance, he knows more about Konrad Milch's murder than either Wendt or Bergemann or anyone else does at this point. So why not see what he's turned up?'

'Yeah, yeah,' said Reineke. 'But a lot of what he knows is stuff we don't want to get out.'

'Well, as I say,' said Gruber, 'as long as he's ours, it won't get out or he's screwed. He knows about the connections between Baron von Plottwietz and the department, for instance.' This made Reineke give Gruber a hard look. 'But he's got to sit on it, as long as he's a cop. And remember, as long as he keeps breaking rules and going off the reservation, he makes it easy for us to get rid of him when the moment is right. And his investigations . . . die with him.'

'*Die* with him? Goddamn it, Sergeant,' said Reineke. Was Gruber talking about killing Geismeier?

'Just a figure of speech, Captain,' said Gruber.

Reineke was no strategic thinker; he was blinded by his grandiose notions. Gruber, on the other hand, had none of Reineke's baggage. He didn't believe in *anything*, other than the pursuit of his own advantage.

Willi had been mulling over the close relationship between Gruber and Reineke for some time. And then it dawned on him. They both knew he had been snooping around cases he had been ordered off. And yet, except for Gruber's occasional little outbursts, Willi had never been disciplined for it. It was almost as though they . . . The hair on the back of Willi's neck stood up.

He was still there when Sergeant Hermann Gruber returned to his office late that same afternoon and found Willi removing the mountain of papers and files from his desk into boxes.

'Well, finally! Geismeier,' he said. 'It's about time you cleaned up that mess.'

'Yes, sir,' said Willi.

'Carry on then,' said Gruber, and went into his office and closed the door.

THE PEOPLE'S COURT

Judge Georg Neidhardt was so preoccupied with the upcoming trial, his soup had gone cold. No surprise that he could think of little else: this was going to be the trial of his career. 'Take the soup away, Karl,' he said. Karl did as he was told.

Every Friday at seven, Georg had his dinner at Concordia, which had been his club since university days. Forty years later he still put on the blue cap and the blue and white sash for all the ceremonial moments and special celebrations. He sang the songs with gusto. Some Concordiens needed sheet music but Georg knew all the songs by heart. Concordia was his life. He considered his Concordia dueling scars – the nick in his ear, the line across his chin – badges of honor. Just as the song said, Concordia was a snug harbor in storm-tossed seas. The high stone walls and iron gate out front, the massive oak doors, the uniformed porter monitoring those who came in, and even Karl, who had been serving at Concordia nearly as long as Georg had been a member, represented safety and security and constant comfort.

Though the dining room was crowded Friday evenings, Georg always ate alone, always at the same table, always the same meal, always with Karl serving. '*Voilà, mein Herr.*' Karl lifted the silver cover from the platter with a flourish. The herring shimmered in cream sauce, nestled between the boiled and buttered potatoes and the red cabbage. Karl poured a splash of Gewürztraminer and waited while Georg took a sip.

'Excellent, Karl,' said Georg. 'Excellent.'

Karl filled the glass.

'*Guten Abend*, Herr Neidhardt,' said the elder of the two men passing the table.

'*Und einen guten Appetit*,' said the other. He clicked his heels and made a crisp little bow. They paused. Georg was about to stand but the older man, Professor Doctor Eberhardt Voss, an eminent judge and university professor, held his hand up to indicate he shouldn't.

Georg was pleased. Voss had never taken much notice of him

before. 'We don't want to interrupt, Herr Neidhardt,' he said. 'Join us in the billiards room for brandy and a cigar afterwards, won't you? We want to hear all about it.' They meant the trial, of course.

Georg Neidhardt had a reputation as a strict defender of order and a stern enforcer of the law against anyone who tried to undermine German civilization and German values. He had recently sent the editor of the *Neue Zeitung*, the Communist newspaper, to prison for 'incitement to class warfare', a vague but convenient charge. After all, almost anything could be called incitement. He had similarly imposed sentences on leftist provocateurs when they had called for a general strike. The strike had not taken place, but to his way of thinking, that didn't diminish the seditious nature of their act. They all went to prison for two years.

On the other hand, when a young fascist assassinated a socialist member of the Reichstag, Georg was convinced that the assassin's love of the German Fatherland and understandable disgust at the member's treachery had driven the young patriot to take extreme measures. The assassin was sentenced to a short imprisonment which was then immediately commuted.

The Bavarian Minister of Justice had determined that Georg Neidhardt would be the perfect judge to preside at the trial of Adolf Hitler and his ten co-conspirators – General Ludendorff and the others – for their abortive uprising the previous November. The charge was treason, violation of Article 81 of the German Penal Code, which stated that anyone attempting to alter by force the constitution of the German Reich should be sentenced to death.

The Putsch had caught the world's attention, and by now, a few months later, interest in the trial was so great that it had to be held in a large hall at the old Infantry School in Blutenburgstraße just to accommodate the huge press contingent. Even so, some had to listen from outside the doors. Sophie, covering it for the *Post*, found herself sitting inside beside a reporter from *The New York Times*.

'How did Ludendorff turn into such a clown?' the *Times* reporter said.

'Don't worry about him,' said Sophie. 'Keep your eye on Adolf Hitler.'

Georg Neidhardt, distinguished in a red robe and black hat, sat with three lay judges beside him on the raised dais. Bailiffs stood behind and beside them to keep order. Georg opened the trial in his usual meticulous and ceremonious way. But once the procedural business was over – the opening, the reading of the charges, the pleas by the accused – he seemed to abandon normal procedure altogether and all but invited Hitler to take over the trial.

Hitler made a long and grandiose opening statement that went on without interruption from either the judge or the prosecution. He was permitted to act as his own attorney, to cross-examine witnesses called by the prosecution and to call his own witnesses. He did not dispute the facts of the Putsch or even the charge that he had committed treason. But it was treason against an illegitimate and evil government, he argued, which not only excused it but made it necessary. There were moments when Judge Neidhardt did find it necessary to interrupt for procedural reasons, but he did so in the most respectful and solicitous manner. 'Herr Hitler, you should perhaps consider . . .' That sort of thing.

Hitler proclaimed himself destined by fate to be Germany's dictator and redeemer. He was the only man who could solve Germany's great and difficult problems, he said, and who could lead the country to its destined greatness. 'Our army of followers grows day by day,' he said. He stood erect, his shoulders back, his chin thrust forward defiantly. He rolled his eyes. He clenched his fists. His voice broke from great emotion. His eyes glistened with tears of conviction. He pressed his fists against his chest in a show of utter sincerity.

'Even now I have the firm conviction that one day the hour will come when these unruly bands of our followers will grow into battalions, the battalions into regiments, and the regiments into divisions, when the old banners will be raised out of the mud and will once again wave before us: and the reconciliation will come in that eternal final Court of Judgment, the Court of God, before which we are ready to stand. Then, from our bones, from our graves, will sound the voice of that tribunal which alone has the right to sit in judgment over us.'

Hitler pointed toward the judges. '*Meine Herren*,' he said, 'it is not *you* who will pronounce final judgment upon us. It is the eternal Court of History that will make its pronouncement upon *you*, upon the charge which is brought against us.

'I already know what your verdict will be. But it does not concern me. That high court will not ask us, "Did you commit high treason or did you not?" *That* court will judge us as Germans who wanted the best for their people and their Fatherland, who wanted to fight and to die. You may pronounce us guilty a thousand times, but the goddess who presides over the Eternal Court of History will, with a smile, tear to pieces the charge of the public prosecutor and the verdict of this court. She will acquit us.'

There were cheers and clapping and stamping feet. 'Jesus,' said the man from the *New York Times*.

Hitler was found guilty of treason, which by law called for the death penalty. Instead he was sentenced to five years in prison with the possibility of early parole. He was escorted from the courtroom to cheers and a chorus of 'Heil, Hitler,' and driven to the prison in Landsberg am Lech, some sixty-five kilometers west of Munich. There he was welcomed like a hero. His cell was comfortably furnished and had windows on two sides. He had books and papers brought to him and almost immediately began receiving visitors bearing gifts. Landsberg was, Hitler said later, his 'state paid university'.

THE BLACK HAND

Fedor Blaskowitz, the Latin teacher, was summoned by the high-school secretary to the conference room. His last class of the day had just ended. 'Herr Blaskowitz,' she said, 'this gentleman is from the police. He would like to speak with you.' She left the two men alone. Willi identified himself and they shook hands.

'I already talked to the police,' said Fedor. He was small, with thinning hair, thick glasses, and a pencil mustache. Though he had claimed to be with Konrad Milch when he was shot, he was not one of the men Willi had seen in the cafe or in the English Garden. And Willi judged immediately that he was not a man that was likely ever to have associated with Milch.

'I know I'm not the first,' said Willi. He tapped the sheaf of papers in his hand. 'I've studied their report. Still, there are just a few things we need to clarify, if you don't mind.'

'I told the police everything I know,' said Fedor. He adjusted his glasses. 'I don't think there's anything I can add to what I already said.'

'Probably not,' said Willi, opening the papers and taking a pencil from his pocket. 'But we've got these procedures we have to go through in every case. A pain, but we've got to do it or the captain has a fit. You understand, I'm sure,' said Willi with a friendly wink and a nod of his head in the direction of the principal's office. Willi touched the pencil to his tongue. 'So, you were with Konrad Milch when he was attacked and shot?'

'Yes, I was there.'

'And there were three of you including Herr Milch?'

'I told the two detectives already,' said Fedor.

'And the third man was?'

'Dieter Hoffmeister. I've already . . .'

'And how many attackers were there?' said Willi.

Fedor sighed in resignation. 'Two. As I said. *Two.*'

'And they attacked you how?'

'What do you mean, "how"?' Fedor was becoming impatient.

'With fists? With clubs? With an iron bar?'

'One of them shot us, that's how, for . . .'

'They didn't attack you first with clubs or anything before they shot you?'

'No. They just shot us.'

'They didn't shoot *you*, or Hoffmeister, did they?'

'No,' said Fedor. 'They didn't *hit* me, but they shot and missed.'

This was an embellishment of Fedor's earlier version, and you could see Fedor wished he hadn't said it. Willi made a note but didn't say anything.

'So, what can you tell me about the two men that attacked you?'

'They were tall, strong. They wore caps low over their eyes.'

'Caps . . . over . . . their . . . eyes,' Willi wrote. 'Was one of them a woman?'

'A woman? What do you mean?'

'It's a simple question: was one of your attackers a woman?'

'Of course not.'

'Are you sure? Because we went over the scene pretty carefully, and one set of footprints definitely belonged to a woman. How do you explain that?'

Fedor had been briefed on what story to tell, and had told it, when prompted, to Detectives Bergemann and Wendt. But he wasn't prepared to answer questions from a persistent investigator, much less one who had studied the crime scene. 'I can't explain it,' he said. 'I only know what I saw.'

'What about the lead pipe that was found at the scene of the crime? And the gun that Konrad Milch was carrying? Did you know there were two guns – the one that shot Milch and the one Milch was carrying?'

'That's not possible,' said Fedor, and regretted saying it in the same moment. 'I didn't see any gun, except for the one that shot Konrad Milch.'

'Not possible? So, you've seen the police report?'

'No, I just meant . . .' He didn't finish the thought.

'Oh, there was a second gun at the scene, all right, Herr Blaskowitz. It belonged to Konrad Milch. It was in his pocket. And there was also a lead pipe. But *you* weren't there, were you?'

'What do you mean?' said Blaskowitz.

'I mean you weren't there. I know you said you were, but you weren't. Were you?'

No answer.

'I see you're an intelligent and educated man, Herr Blaskowitz. You've been to university. You've studied the classics. You know what it means to impede a police investigation, don't you? And you probably have some idea of the penalties for doing so.'

Again Fedor didn't answer.

'Well, then, let me remind you. Obstructing justice – preventing the police from doing their job – is a very serious crime. The *minimum* penalty for obstruction of justice is five years in prison.'

Fedor tried one more time. 'I don't know what you're talking about.'

Willi gave him a long, appraising look, then finally nodded his head. 'I see,' he said. 'Have it your way.' He took handcuffs from his coat pocket. 'Please turn around, Herr Blaskowitz.'

Fedor suddenly had tears in his eyes. 'Please,' he said.

'Who told you to say what you have said?'

'Please,' he said again.

'I see you're in a bind, Herr Blaskowitz. I'd like to help you, I really would. But I can't unless you're willing to help yourself by telling me the truth.' He let the cuffs dangle from his hand. 'Who told you to give false testimony? The police – Wendt and Bergemann?'

'Yes . . . No . . . I'll lose my job . . . I'll . . .'

'Someone else then.'

There was a perfunctory knock at the door, which opened. Willi slid the cuffs into his pocket. 'Everything all right in here, Blaskowitz?' A pale, squat man with a shaved head came into the room. 'I'm Dr Bruck, the school principal, Detective. The secretary told me you were here. Is everything all right?'

'Of course,' said Willi. 'I'm just confirming Mr Blaskowitz's earlier witness statement. Everything checks out.'

'I'm not surprised,' said Dr Bruck. 'Blaskowitz is an excellent fellow, good character, honest, all that. Right, Blaskowitz?'

'Yes, sir,' said Willi. 'I see that.'

Fedor said nothing.

'Well, Detective, I'll leave you to it then,' said Dr Bruck. He turned slightly and extended his left hand toward Willi instead of his right, which hung uselessly at his side, encased in a black glove.

Once Dr Bruck had left, Willi lay the handcuffs on the table. He motioned for Fedor to have a seat. He sat down across the table and for a long time seemed to study his notes. 'How long have you been here at the Herder Gymnasium, Herr Blaskowitz?' Fedor had been gazing at the handcuffs, and the sound of Willi's voice startled him. 'How long?'

Willi waited.

'Three years,' said Fedor.

'And was it Dr Bruck who hired you?'

'Yes,' said Fedor.

'And what do you know about him?'

'Know about *him*? Dr Bruck?' Fedor appeared not to like the turn their conversation had taken.

Fedor was a timid soul, in love with the Greek and Latin classics. But he was awkward and inept and unable to impart that love to the young men in his charge. From his first day there three years earlier he had been the almost constant victim of student pranks. Every school seems to have one such unfortunate teacher who, through no fault of his own, becomes the designated target, the butt of student abuse. Fedor had been tormented cruelly. Eventually he stopped responding to their torture and went through the day like a man in a trance. One day, for no apparent reason, the students decided that torturing him was no longer as amusing as it had been, and that Fedor should be gotten rid of. The ringleader of the students, a boy named Schneidermann, told Dr Bruck that Fedor had made sexual overtures toward him. Dr Bruck knew the boy was lying, but also recognized the opportunity it presented.

'These things can happen, Blaskowitz,' said Dr Bruck. 'Schneidermann is a handsome young fellow. We'll say no more about it.' Fedor now owed Dr Bruck everything, and that would, Bruck was certain, be useful to him. When Captain Reineke told Bruck he was looking for a 'witness', Dr Bruck said, 'I've got just the man.'

'Is he reliable?' Reineke wondered. 'What are his politics?'

'His politics don't matter,' said Dr Bruck. 'And he's completely reliable.'

'I did nothing with Schneidermann, or any other student,' Fedor told Willi now. 'But I am . . . I am not inclined toward women. So . . .'

'So he had you.'

'Yes,' said Fedor. 'He had me. He told me police were coming to interview me, and he told me what to say.'

'Had you been given their questions in advance?'

'No. Just the story to tell.'

'Did you have the sense that the police had been given their questions in advance?'

'I don't know. I don't think so.'

'Did they read them or improvise them?'

'They didn't read them. Although they seemed very uncurious about my answers and didn't ask any follow-up questions. I remember thinking that was odd. But I was relieved.'

'Did anyone tell you anything about the crime being investigated?'

'Dr Bruck told me a patriot had been shot down in cold blood and the villain was likely to get away with it unless a witness could be found. I was . . . *am* that witness. Dr Bruck is an enthusiastic patriot. He lost his hand in the war.'

'And it didn't bother you that you were giving false testimony?'

'Of course it did, but I didn't see that I had any choice.'

'And do you see any choice now?'

Tears sprang to Fedor's eyes again. 'No, I don't. I'm finished, washed up.'

'Listen to me,' said Willi, picking up the cuffs and sliding them into his pocket. 'If you cooperate with me, you *will* have a choice. Dr Bruck will never know from me or anyone else what you've told me, and he must never know from you. Neither must Bergemann or Wendt, the two detectives you talked to. Just stick to the testimony you already gave them. It will stand in the official record.'

'Is someone being framed? I could never live with that.'

'I can't tell you any more about this case than I already have,' said Willi. 'I suppose Dr Bruck will ask you about our interview.'

'I'm sure he will. What should I say?'

Willi thought for a moment. 'Let him know that the police suspect Konrad Milch, the man who was killed, of having been involved in the bombing of a newspaper more than two years back.'

'Is that true?' said Blaskowitz, his face going pale.

'I can't say anything more about it,' said Willi. 'Just let him know you learned from me that Milch is suspected of the bombing of a newspaper.'

'How do I do that?'

'Just say, "The detective thinks that Konrad Milch bombed a newspaper." That's all.'

'Will he ask me anything about that?'

'If he does, just say that's all I said about it.'

'I don't understand any of this,' said Fedor. 'One policeman says Milch is a victim and a hero, and another says he's a killer. How is anyone to make sense of it?'

'There's no making sense of it, Herr Blaskowitz. It's the times we live in. There are two kinds of police now, two kinds of truth, and two kinds of justice. There is true justice and false justice that twists the truth. Nowadays in Munich, more and more often official justice is false; more and more often the law is on the side of false justice. True justice is inconvenient and difficult and dangerous. It's the kind of justice that gets trampled on, that doesn't get a hearing, that is often suppressed or withheld. I'm afraid that the law has moved to the dark side, Herr Blaskowitz.'

ROSENCRANTZ AND GUILDENSTERN

Detectives Robert Wendt and Hans Bergemann had not been partners very long. But from the first day of their partnership they had found an almost instant rapport with one another, the ease that usually arrives only after a long friendship. It did not hurt that the two men were in political agreement. Both were attracted to National Socialism, but in a casual way, without having given it much thought. They liked the idea of reviving German traditions, strengthening the family, making Germany great again, feeling good about things again. What could be wrong with that? They were stirred by Hitler's evocation of a golden future that was much like the golden German past. They loved the folksiness, the *Gemütlichkeit*: stirring speeches and uniforms and parades, Sunday walks in the country, their wives in dirndl, singing the old songs, a good *Jägerschnitzel* and a large *Hofbräu*, a meerschaum pipe by the fire. You might have called them armchair Nazis, and neither man would have objected too strenuously.

Both men thought alike about their work. Willi was right: they were lazy. They pursued evidence in a lackadaisical way, following the easy leads that led where they wanted to go. They interrogated witnesses in a superficial manner so as not to turn up any uncomfortable surprises. Being partnered with someone whose work habits mirror your own only reinforces and confirms you in your ways. Before long, they were finishing one another's sentences like an old married couple. *Rosencrantz and Guildenstern*, thought Willi. He was still visited by Shakespeare when it was appropriate. '*I will trust them as I will adders fang'd.*' That was Hamlet.

The case file that had come down from Gruber listed Dieter Hoffmeister and Fedor Blaskowitz as the two principal witnesses.

'Let's start with Blaskowitz?' said Wendt.

'Yes, by all means,' said Bergemann.

Blaskowitz, shy, even timid, seemed to both men an unlikely witness. But his answers to their inquiries, while not exactly compelling – they seemed rehearsed and lacked specificity – confirmed the detective sergeant's instincts, as he had laid them out. So the detectives were satisfied, for the moment at least.

According to Blaskowitz, he and Hoffmeister and Konrad Milch had been walking in the English Garden, where they were attacked. No, he couldn't identify either of the attackers; they wore caps pulled low over their faces. No, they hadn't demanded money. One of them had attacked Konrad Milch verbally, calling him a Nazi asshole, and had then pulled out a gun and shot him. He and Hoffmeister had then run away.

'Do you have any idea why they attacked Milch? Did they know him?' Wendt said.

'I had the feeling they knew him,' said Blaskowitz. 'An artist from the *Post* had a show of his drawings in an art gallery nearby. He had made a drawing of Milch. Milch didn't like it, and it was in the show. And the artist had published that drawing in the *Post*. It was like he had it in for Konrad. Maybe he was one of the attackers.'

Wendt asked for the name of the gallery. Bergemann asked for the artist's name. Fedor recalled both names; neither detective found it odd that he did. Wendt asked whether Milch and the artist had met before that evening? Fedor didn't know whether they had met before. But they must have, if the artist had been able to draw him.

'How long have you known the victim?' said Wendt.

'Not very long,' said Blaskowitz.

'Where did you meet?' said Bergemann.

'I don't remember.'

Wendt and Bergemann decided to interview Hoffmeister next and then find the artist, Maximilian Wolf. Hoffmeister worked at National Socialist headquarters as a custodian and maintenance man. Wendt and Bergemann had never been to the Party head-quarters before. The building was heavily guarded. Hoffmeister was small and skinny with a pockmarked face and an Adam's apple that bobbed up and down as he spoke. But he stood in the hall with his feet spread and his thumbs hooked over his belt as though he owned the place. His answers echoed Blaskowitz's. 'A little too much, don't you think?' said Wendt.

'Absolutely,' said Bergemann. 'They used almost the same words.' The detectives were lazy but not stupid.

The artist Maximilian Wolf had his work in the *Post* several times a week, so it was easy enough to look him up.

'What do you think?' said Bergemann.

'I wouldn't want this guy to draw my picture,' said Wendt, looking at Maximilian's latest drawings.

'I know what you mean,' said Bergemann. 'But if he did, so what? Would you be that upset about it? I mean, it's just a picture.'

'Let's go talk to him,' said Wendt.

They found Maximilian at the *Post*. 'We won't keep you long,' said Bergemann.

'How well did you know the deceased?' said Wendt.

'I didn't know him at all,' said Maximilian.

'But you drew him,' said Bergemann. 'Why?'

'I was doing drawings at the Nazi march – I'm paid to do drawings of goings-on around the city. He had an interesting face. That's all.'

'Interesting?' said Wendt.

'What do you mean?' said Bergemann.

'It wasn't just a face. It expressed violent emotions,' said Maximilian. 'That was interesting.'

'He was marching past you that day. It can't have taken more than a few seconds for him to pass. If you didn't know him, how could you draw him so quickly?'

'I draw quickly, because I have to,' said Maximilian. 'It's how I work. I make quick notes. Then, if I need to, I can refine the drawing later.'

'Show me,' said Wendt.

Maximilian did a quick drawing of Bergemann. He caught his unruly hair, his large ears, his scowling eyes and downturned mouth in a few lines. He showed the men his drawing. Wendt laughed. Bergemann continued to scowl as he studied the drawing. He could see how being drawn could make you angry. 'Where were you on the night in question?' he said.

'I was at the Appelbaum Gallery until after eleven, then I went home.'

'Can anyone vouch for you?' said Bergemann.

'I was with my partner. Sophie Auerbach.'

They wrote down the name and address.

'What do you think?' said Wendt as they left the offices of the *Post*.

Bergemann was still scowling at his portrait. Maximilian had given it to him, after promising not to put it in the paper. 'It makes me look old,' he said.

Wendt laughed. 'Not about the drawing, man. What do you think about Wolf as a suspect?'

'I don't know. He's hiding something. But then, everybody's hiding something.'

'Yeah, I agree. We should talk to the girlfriend.'

THE GUN

Sophie had applied for a permit to carry a pistol and, because of her dangerous work, had received one. After she shot Konrad, Willi threw the Luger into the Isar. He watched as it sank from sight. 'Get another one,' he said, and she did. *Post* reporters received threatening calls and letters all the time. Sophie was as used to being under constant threat as one can be.

But killing a man, shooting him and watching him die, hit her harder than she might have expected. She didn't want to carry a gun again; she wanted nothing more to do with guns. She wanted to research Konrad Milch, to find out what she could about him, about his life and family. Maximilian did his best to discourage this. 'Please, don't,' he said. 'You won't learn anything that will make what happened easier to live with. You'll learn, whatever he did, there were still those who loved him and will miss him.'

'Irena,' she said.

'Yes. Maybe Irena,' he said.

So, when Bergemann and Wendt asked to interview her, she agreed to meet the detectives at her office. But even in that safe place, she felt uneasy in a way she could not conceal.

'Remember,' Willi had told her, 'the police don't know anything about that evening.'

'They don't know we were there,' said Maximilian.

Still, she was nervous.

'Miss Auerbach,' said Bergemann as the very first thing, 'do you own a gun?'

'Yes,' said Sophie.

'Do you have a license?'

'Yes,' she said.

'Could we see the gun and the license?'

It was a small Derringer. They smelled the gun and studied the license.

'Why do you need a gun?' said Wendt.

'For protection,' she said.

'Have you been attacked?' said Bergemann.

Sophie looked at him in astonishment. 'Do you consider being blown up being attacked?'

'What do you mean?' said Wendt.

'It must be in your files. I worked at *Das Neue Deutsche Bild* when it was bombed. I was sitting with my editor, Erwin Czieslow, when a hand grenade was rolled into the office. He and another man were killed. I was badly injured and spent many months in the hospital. Are you really unaware of any of this?'

It was evident that they were. Wendt and Bergemann looked at one another, then rifled through the papers in front of them to discover whether there was any mention of this major fact. There was none. Their lack of preparation for the interview made them look like fools, and they were plainly embarrassed. Sophie could have been indignant, but instead she chose the wiser course, which was to fill in the blanks in their understanding in such a way as to elicit not just their sympathy, but also their gratitude for not rubbing their noses in their ineptitude.

'She doesn't appear to have anything to do with the murder,' said Wendt.

'I think that's probably the case,' said Bergemann. 'And she gives Maximilian Wolf an alibi too.'

'Still,' said Wendt, 'she has a gun.'

'Let's check the permits and see if there are any other guns,' said Bergemann.

THE LONG LEASH

Hermann Gruber had engineered a rise through the police and detective ranks with what could be called brilliant cynicism. He had taken advantage of the political moment to get where he was now, a detective sergeant in charge of a squad. His father would have been proud and amazed. And now he was ready to take the next step and go even higher. Only one thing stood in his way.

Hermann's wife of ten years, Mitzi, whom he loved dearly, and who loved him, had parents, Werner and Anna Schwarz (née Flegenheim), living in an apartment in the southern outskirts of the city. On a clear day they had a view of the Alps. Mitzi had recently begun paying them weekly visits. And lately she seemed moodier, at least to Hermann. 'What is it, Mitzi?' Hermann asked. 'What's bothering you?'

'*Vati* and *Mutti* are getting old,' she said. 'That's all.' But both Anna and Werner were robust and active. They worked long hours in their orchard and garden, and showed no sign of slowing down.

It wasn't that they were getting old. It was that they, or rather she, Anna, was Jewish, which made Mitzi half-Jewish. Mitzi was not blind. She saw the anti-Semitic graffiti when she went out for groceries or just took a walk. She read about attacks on Jews and Jewish shops.

She watched Hermann in front of the mirror each morning, adjusting his brown uniform, the same uniform some of the men making these attacks wore. He tightened the knot in his tie, smoothing it against his stomach. 'Mitz,' he said. 'There's a wrinkle. See it?' He pointed. 'I can't have that. I'm going with the captain on his rounds today.'

She turned and walked from the room. He followed her. 'Iron it yourself,' she said.

'What? What's gotten into you, Mitz?'

She didn't answer, and Hermann knew better than to push it. He gave the wrinkle another look. 'It'll have to do,' he muttered, and went off to work.

Hermann didn't think of Mitzi as Jewish; he thought of her as German. So had she, for that matter, until recently. She had never in her life been inside a synagogue, never celebrated Passover, hardly even knew what Passover was. And yet, people just like her had been attacked, were still being attacked, even though the times were supposedly better. She'd asked Hermann about it once. 'Did you investigate when that Jewish jewelry store was attacked?' 'Of course not,' he'd said, a little too gruffly. 'We have more serious crimes. We're overloaded with work.' Hermann must have known the moment would come when his career and Mitzi would collide.

After making the rounds with Captain Reineke, Hermann returned to the office to find Willi working at his desk. Hermann had used Reineke to get where he was and then cultivated other connections which were about to pay off. But Reineke believed in all that Aryan stuff. He made cracks to Hermann about Jews on the force and how, one day, they would all be gone. 'Is Geismeier a Jew?' Reineke said one morning.

'I don't know, sir,' said Hermann.

'That seems like something you would want to know about the people under you, Detective Sergeant. Especially someone like Geismeier.'

'Yes, sir,' said Hermann.

'You've still got a tail on him, I hope.'

'Yes, sir.'

Word had come down that Hitler was organizing a brand-new security unit, a sort of elite guard, called the Schutzstaffel, the SS. Reineke had told Hermann Gruber he was being considered for membership. Membership required loyalty to Hitler, which was no problem, and a clean record, also no problem. But you also needed a clean racial history. Which brought Mitzi into the picture.

Since Reineke had made him a sergeant, Hermann had looked mainly to pleasing his superiors, and had treated the detectives under him with indifference. He had assumed Wendt and Bergemann were reliable, but were they? Why would they be? What had he ever done for them? And Geismeier. He had a tail on Geismeier, that Geismeier certainly knew about. Geismeier was the smartest one of the bunch.

Hermann suddenly felt isolated and vulnerable. 'Geismeier, do you have a minute?' he said, calling from his office door.

'Detective Sergeant?'

'Do you have a minute? Could you please come in?'

'Yes, sir,' said Willi, closing the file he had been studying, putting it in the desk drawer and locking it.

Gruber gestured toward the chair facing his desk and Willi sat down. 'Cigarette?' He held out his case toward Willi.

'No thank you, Sergeant. I don't smoke.'

I didn't even know that *about him*, thought Gruber. 'How's your wife, Geismeier? I don't think I've ever had the pleasure.'

'No, sir, I don't think so. She's fine. Thank you for asking.'

Gruber hadn't even known for sure whether Willi had a wife, so that had worked out all right. Or had it? *Did* he have a wife, or was he lying? You never could tell with Geismeier.

'Are congratulations in order, Detective Sergeant?' said Willi. 'If so let me be the first.'

How the devil did Willi know about the SS thing? It hadn't even been approved yet. 'Yes, thank you, Geismeier. That's kind of you.'

'What can I do for you, Detective Sergeant?' said Willi.

'We haven't caught up in some time, Geismeier. I just wanted you to bring me up to date on what you're working on.'

Willi listed three cases and gave brief summaries of each. One was an attack on an Orthodox Jewish family, but Hermann wanted to give that one a wide berth, and he hardly knew enough about the other two cases – both house break-ins – to ask any questions. 'And what about the murder of Konrad Milch, Geismeier?'

'You ordered me off that case, sir.'

'But you've continued to investigate, despite my order, haven't you?' He said it in what was meant to be a jocular tone.

'No, sir.'

'Well, damn it, Geismeier, I've heard that you were talking about the case, planting rumors . . .'

'If that's Blaskowitz you're asking about, that was before your order, sir. And I wasn't planting anything. I was giving him a little misinformation, trying to get him to make contact with Hoffmeister, the other witness. Just to see where that might lead. Trying to sow a little panic, Detective Sergeant.'

'I see. And did it? Sow panic, I mean?'

'Well, you've heard from him, so it seems to have done something. You *did* hear from him, didn't you, sir?'

'Not exactly,' said Hermann.

'Well then, from Dr Bruck,' said Willi.

'Never mind about that. Let's get back to that Jewish case of yours for a moment.' This suddenly seemed like safer territory.

'Jewish case?' said Willi.

'The attack on the Jewish family. How are you dealing with that one, Geismeier?'

'I've interviewed the family. There were several witnesses, and I'm interviewing them as well. I'm not sure I understand your question, sir.'

'Well, they *are* Jewish, Geismeier. I'm just wondering whether you're doing anything . . . different there.'

'*Should* I be doing something different, Detective Sergeant?'

'Of course not, Geismeier. I mean, just give it your full attention. Like you would any other case.'

'Is there something you'd like me do that I'm not doing, sir? I'm always happy to get your guidance.'

That cheeky little bastard, thought Hermann. 'No, Geismeier, that's not what I meant. Continue what you've been doing. And stay away from the Milch shooting.'

'Milch?'

'Damn it! The young patriot killed in the park.'

'Oh, yes, sir,' said Willi. 'The young patriot. Will that be all?'

'Yes, thank you, Geismeier. And my best regards to your wife.'

'Thank you, sir. Shall I close the door?'

Once he was alone, Hermann groaned. It felt like he had just been interrogated by his own detective.

THE RIVER ISAR

Since she had shot and killed Konrad Milch, Sophie was fearful and distraught. She was afraid to go out alone. She withdrew into herself. She couldn't eat or sleep. She didn't want to see anyone. Elizabeth Grynbaum knocked at the door, but Sophie didn't answer. Not even for Elizabeth who had become like a mother to her. Maximilian assured Sophie the incident was just that – an incident – and it was over. He could think that way because he had killed men in the war. He reminded her she had saved his life. But it didn't help.

Then one morning it was as though the fever broke. The killing of Milch was still on her mind, but it had become a kind of admonition, a reminder of the danger National Socialism had presented for her, and also for all of Germany. It helped too that everybody else seemed to think the National Socialist moment was past. Even some editors at the *Post* argued for giving the Nazis less space in the paper. The Nazis were a laughing stock, they said. The threat was over. More important stories were getting short shrift because of the *Post*'s Nazi fixation. France's and then Japan's recognition of the Soviet Union were certainly important stories. The Soviet Union, a dangerous regime, was gaining legitimacy from day to day, and yet that had barely gotten a mention in the paper. Even the machinations within the Bavarian government were being neglected.

Maximilian's successful show at the Appelbaum Gallery and the sale of many drawings had allowed Maximilian and Sophie to move from Elizabeth Grynbaum's narrow bedroom to an apartment across the landing. They now had a large modern kitchen, with an ice box and a new gas stove, a full bathroom, and two bedrooms. They used the bedroom with its skylight as their office and studio. They worked across from one another at a massive oak table – it had taken four men to get it up the stairs and into place. Sophie clattered away on her typewriter. Maximilian liked the noise; to him it was the sound of happiness.

He had spread out several dozen drawings on his side of the table and then on the floor and chairs, wherever there was space. He was beginning to put together a show for the coming winter at Appelbaum's Berlin gallery and needed to narrow the number to fifty.

'Can you take a break?' he said. 'Come help me with this.' He steered Sophie past the drawings he had laid out.

'Not this one,' she said. 'But all of these should go.' She pointed to the series of drawings he had made in clubs and cabarets around the city, leering men and half-dressed women. Most were starkly drawn with slashing black lines and sharp angles. The perspective was skewed, and in some he had added a touch of color – a dash of red on a mouth, a blueish nose, pale yellow sagging flesh.

Sophie also liked the movie series. Maximilian had happened on a crew making a film in the old city. There were trucks and lights and cranes and dollies crowded into the narrow street. Cables snaked this way and that. Maximilian did drawings of actors, including Emil Jannings and Pola Negri, in medieval dress. He drew the crew. His likenesses of Fritz Murnau, the director, Jannings and Negri ran in the Sunday edition. Sophie liked the portraits. 'They'll be good in Berlin,' she said. She especially liked the drawings of the crew, bored, smoking while they waited to shoot the next scene, or moving equipment around. In one drawing Murnau peered through a square opening he made with his hands. Sophie laced her arm through Maximilian's and pointed to other drawings she would choose. Neither Sophie nor Maximilian had ever expected such happiness or good fortune.

It was late on a September afternoon. The windows were open. The sound of traffic came in on a warm breeze that tossed the lace curtains this way and that. Sophie was alone. There was a knock at the door. She looked through the peephole and recognized Wendt and Bergemann. Bergemann leaned in and knocked again. Sophie opened the door.

The two policemen introduced themselves, in case she had forgotten who they were. No, she said, she hadn't. Could they come in? they wondered, although they were both already halfway through the door when they asked. Sophie stepped aside and gestured toward the kitchen, which was the first room you came to. She invited them to sit down and offered them tea, which they declined.

The two men looked around and nodded approvingly. 'This is a very nice apartment, Fräulein. Congratulations.'

'What is it you want?' she said.

They both looked shocked, as though they had really meant to pay her a compliment.

'We're here about Konrad Milch,' said Wendt.

Sophie's heart began to pound. 'Who?' said Sophie.

'We spoke with you about him some time back,' said Bergemann. 'You remember.'

'The man who was shot in the English Garden,' said Wendt.

'Oh, yes,' she said. 'What about him?'

'Well, Fräulein, you probably recall that the last time we spoke, we weren't aware that you had been . . . attacked, which had led you to apply for a gun license and to carry a gun for your own protection.'

'Which is understandable,' said Wendt.

'We went back and checked your story,' said Bergemann.

'And found it to be true,' said Wendt. 'But then we also checked to see whether you had owned any other guns. It came to light then that you *had* owned another gun.'

'A Luger. Fully legal and licensed, of course,' said Bergemann.

'But the thing is,' said Wendt, 'the gun that killed Konrad Milch could have been a Luger.'

'We think it could have been *your* Luger, Fräulein Auerbach,' said Bergemann, and immediately regretted saying it.

'We'd like to close this case, Fräulein,' said Wendt, trying to hurry past Bergemann's blunder.

'Could we see the gun, please, and your permit?' said Bergemann.

'Do you have a warrant, either for my arrest or to search my home?' said Sophie.

'No, Fräulein, we don't,' said Bergemann. 'But your refusal makes me wonder what you might have to hide.'

'We can come back with a search warrant and a forensic team, if that's what you want,' said Wendt. 'Then your beautiful apartment is liable to be turned upside down. Our officers are not always as careful in their searches as my partner and I would like them to be.'

'I don't have the Luger,' said Sophie.

'Where is it?' said Bergemann.

'I threw it in the Isar.'

'You threw it in the river?' said Wendt.

'I didn't like carrying it, I didn't want to have it any longer, and I couldn't think how else to get rid of it.'

'When did this happen?' said Wendt.

'I don't remember. A while ago.'

'You expect us to believe that?' said Bergemann.

'I don't care whether you believe it or not. Is it a crime to throw away a gun?'

The detectives looked at each other helplessly.

'I want you to leave,' said Sophie.

'Fräulein, I advise you . . .'

'Now,' said Sophie.

As the two men stood up to go, the door opened and Maximilian came in.

'Don't say anything, Maximilian. The detectives are just leaving.'

NEW EVIDENCE

Willi sat at Sophie and Maximilian's kitchen table where Rosencrantz and Guildenstern had sat not too many hours earlier. 'You told them you threw the gun in the river?' said Willi.

'Was that bad?' she asked.

Willi did something he rarely did. He laughed. 'No,' he said. 'It was brilliant.'

'Really? Doesn't it seem like I'm lying?'

'Of course,' said Willi. 'Except it's such an obvious lie, that it must be true. Do you follow me?'

'Not exactly,' said Sophie. She was still shaken. 'Will they come back?' she asked.

'I doubt it. They don't have any evidence,' said Willi, 'and they're not looking for any.'

'They don't have any evidence against me?'

'None,' said Willi. 'Remember, they're not really even investigating. You're not a suspect, you're a scapegoat. They, or more likely their bosses, are trying to frame you.'

'They're trying to frame me for something *I did*?'

'Yeah, well. They don't *know* you did it. And frankly it doesn't matter to them. Remember, what you did was obviously self-defense, and that's easy to prove, when the time comes when we have to.'

'Easy to prove?'

'Milch was a thug and a murderer. His so-called witnesses are lying. And the two guys who were actually with him are in hiding for some reason, so they won't be testifying. But Milch as a murderer and you acting in self-defense runs counter to the story they, or whoever's pulling the strings, want to prove. What they want is to hang a murder charge on you. I'm pretty sure, however, that Bergemann and Wendt don't understand that.'

'So why are they doing it?'

'They're being pushed in that direction. And they're lazy and uncurious,' said Willi.

'And the fact that I actually killed Milch?'

'Would come as a complete surprise to those two, I'm sure.'

'So what should I do?' said Sophie. Her voice broke.

Willi thought for a moment. 'Maybe it's time to make our two cops less uncurious. Let's see if they have any backbone. Do you think you could write a story for the *Post* about the *Deutsche Bild* bombing?'

'Me? No, never. It would have to be someone who wasn't involved in any way.'

'Is there someone who could do it?'

'Sure. But the paper won't print it. It's ancient history.'

'What if there were new evidence?' Willi said.

Two days later a short article appeared in the *Post*, accompanied by the drawing of Konrad Milch that Maximilian had made those years ago with Walther Hinzig's help.

> *New Evidence in Bombing Case*
> *On the morning of December 12, 1921, according to eyewitnesses, two men rolled a hand grenade into the offices of* Das Neue Deutsche Bild, *killing two members of the newspaper's staff and injuring five others. The newspaper was closed permanently not long after the attack. The attackers were never identified or brought to justice.*
>
> *Now, according to police department sources, new evidence has surfaced indicating that Konrad Milch, the recently murdered storm trooper and member of the NSDAP, was one of the bombers. Milch was responsible for many assaults in the course of his brief criminal career. According to well-placed sources, evidence was found after Milch's death on his person and in his home implicating him in the bombing and pointing to his accomplice. Our sources are unwilling to identify the second bomber at this time but suggest that his identity is known to the police and that they are in the process of gathering evidence against him.*

Detective Robert Wendt arrived at the office the next morning to find a copy of the *Post* lying open on his desk. 'I put it there,' said Willi from across the room. 'I didn't know if you'd seen it or not.'

Wendt studied the picture and read the article. 'No, I hadn't seen it. Where did they get this?' said Wendt.

Willi held up his hands. 'No idea,' he said. 'I just thought you'd be interested.'

'You're damn right I am,' said Wendt. He read it again.

'You didn't know?' said Willi.

'No. What do you make of it?' said Wendt.

'Me? I don't make anything of it. Not my business. I'm not going to step on your case.'

'No,' said Wendt. 'But still . . . It's not right.'

'What do you mean?' said Willi.

'Well, if the guy whose murder we're looking into was actually a murderer himself, well, that changes everything, doesn't it?'

'I suppose it might,' said Willi.

'So *somebody*' – he nodded his head in the direction of Gruber's office – 'knew this and didn't tell us.'

'Why would anybody do that?' said Willi.

'Yeah, that's the question, isn't it? Maybe they just wanted us to follow the evidence.' That seemed the easiest explanation.

'Yeah, that *could* be it,' said Willi.

'But you don't think so,' said Wendt, walking over to Willi's desk.

'No, I'm not saying that. Look, Robert, I don't want to horn in on your case.'

'I'm not asking you to. I'm just asking your opinion. What do you think? What would you do in our shoes?'

Willi studied Wendt's face for several seconds. 'OK,' he said, as though, after careful thought, he had decided he could be helpful. 'First of all, I'd want to find out for sure who this guy Milch was. Everything about him. He's obviously not the Boy Scout they're saying he is. Then I'd want to know who they think was with him when he bombed that paper – who's the second guy. Finally, I'd want to know why all this information was withheld from me.'

'And how would you find all this out?'

'I'd ask,' said Willi.

'Gruber?'

'First I'd start with Milch's witnesses – I don't know their names.'

'Blaskowitz and Hoffmeister. What about Gruber? Would you ask him?'

'Is he the one who briefed you on the case?'

'Yeah,' said Wendt.

'Did the story come from him? Or somewhere else?'

'I don't know.' Wendt thought for a moment. 'So you think we were lied to?'

Finally! thought Willi. 'No, I'm not going to say that. I'm sure Gruber had his theories about the case and was just sending you in that direction.'

'We need to talk to Gruber,' said Wendt, more to himself than to Willi.

'You don't want to tell him you talked to me about any of this,' said Willi.

'Are you kidding? You think I'm crazy?' Wendt laughed. 'Gruber *hates* you.'

WENDT AND BERGEMANN

When Hans Bergemann arrived at the office a few minutes later, Wendt tucked the newspaper under his arm, grabbed him, and steered him out of the office. They spent the rest of the morning with Hoffmeister and then Blaskowitz, poking holes in their stories and determining that both men had lied about being with Milch the night of the attack. Neither Hoffmeister nor Blaskowitz was able to shed any light on the newspaper bombing.

Over lunch in a *Gasthaus* far from the station, the two detectives went over the morning's revelations, as well as all the new questions the morning's interviews had raised. 'So, who was *actually* with Milch when he was killed? Where are they and why are they hiding? And why would Hoffmeister and Blaskowitz pretend to be Konrad Milch's sidekicks?'

'Well, they didn't expect they'd be found out,' said Wendt. 'They thought they wouldn't be questioned too hard. Nobody would ever know they were lying, and nobody would be the wiser. They'd give their statements and that would be the end of it. So, they're not just a couple of amateurs doing somebody a favor. Somebody's got something on them. They're both scared. Especially the teacher.'

'We need to push them both harder,' said Bergemann. 'Find out who's behind their story.'

'Not yet,' said Wendt. 'We need to know more about the lay of the land before we push anyone.'

Bergemann lifted his beer to drink and then paused, the tankard in mid-air. 'And what the hell was Milch doing in the English Garden that got him killed?'

'That's the big question, isn't it?' said Wendt. 'If we knew that, then a lot of other stuff would be clear.'

'Well, here's another question,' said Bergemann. 'What's Geismeier got to do with it? What's he getting out of all this?'

'I don't think he's involved. *I* asked *him* for help. He didn't want to be involved. He's scared of Gruber.'

'Oh, come on, Robert,' said Bergemann. 'He gave you the newspaper, for Christ's sake. He's a clever son of a bitch. He knows exactly what he's doing.'

'So then, what's he up to?' said Wendt.

'Well, if I had to guess, I'd say he's playing his own game on some parallel track. Outside the department; outside the system.'

'Why?' said Wendt.

'I don't know, but I'd guess it has to do with Gruber. Or somebody higher up. Reineke, maybe.'

They had all but stopped eating.

'Here's another question for you,' said Wendt. 'Geismeier's the best detective in the unit, maybe in the city, right?'

'Yeah, so?'

'So why hasn't he been promoted? He's been there since the war, and he's still a detective, never been promoted.'

'Well, for one thing, Gruber hates him,' said Bergemann.

'This goes back before Gruber.'

'Yeah, well, Captain Reineke doesn't like him either. Geismeier's always going off on his own. Let's face it, Robert, Willi's a pain in the ass.'

'Yeah, he's a pain in the ass. So then why hasn't he been fired? Or transferred or disciplined? He keeps getting ordered off cases, slapped down by Gruber. How does he stand that? Why doesn't he just quit?'

'Maybe *that's* the parallel track. Maybe he's not actually off the cases.'

'You mean he's working for someone else, for the NSDAP? A Party spy inside the police?'

'Or maybe he's not a spy *for* the Party. Maybe he's a spy *against* the Party.'

'No. That would be a hell of a dangerous game. And who would he be working for?'

'The Communists? The government?'

The two men sat in silence for a long time. Their food sat forgotten in front of them.

'So . . .' said Wendt finally. 'Why's he helping *us*? Or *is* he helping us? Why steer us the way he did, against Gruber's version of what happened to Milch? Which means against the captain, who's a big Nazi? Which means against the Party?'

'So he's using us,' said Bergemann.

'Yeah, but for what? He just steered us *toward* the truth about Milch. He saved us from embarrassing ourselves there. Why?' said Wendt. 'He knows we're for the Party.'

'Come on,' said Bergemann, '*are* we for the Party? Christ, I don't even know *what* I'm for any more. I mean, we're being screwed by the Party we're supposedly part of.'

'Well, we're not actually part of it,' said Wendt. 'We're not members.'

'Maybe we should be. Maybe we should join?' said Bergemann.

'Come on, Hans. We've talked about that. Besides, they're messing with us.'

'Still, it's how you get ahead in the department. Look at Gruber.'

'Yeah, look at him,' said Wendt. 'He looks more and more like a scared rabbit. Think about it for a minute. You've seen it: if you're not with those guys a hundred percent, you're against them. That's the way they think. And they don't screw around.'

'Maybe they're protecting Milch. After all, he was one of them.'

'So whose side are *we* on, Robert? That's the first thing we need to figure out.'

What was left of the sausages was cold, the butter on the potatoes had congealed, the sauerkraut was cold and grey. They pushed their plates away. The waitress came to add up their bill. 'Two *Knackwürstl*, two liters of Hofbräu. Bread?' she asked. They looked at her as though she had just said something in Chinese. 'How many *Brötchen*?' she said again.

'Oh. Two,' said Wendt. He picked up his roll with one bite out of it and looked at it. She added the ten pfennigs, figured the tip, and tallied the total. They paid but didn't leave.

'OK. So again: who were the two men with Milch when he was killed?' said Bergemann. Maybe if they went back to the beginning, something would reveal itself. 'And who was the second bomber?'

'Hey! Maybe the piece in the *Post* will shake the bushes. Let's see who comes running out.'

'And Geismeier. Let's keep watching Geismeier.'

FAMILY HEIRLOOMS

Willi was often followed these days. Today it was Wendt. Willi didn't spot him right away, and when he did he decided to make use of the situation. He was on his way to NSDAP headquarters, so he made it look like he was familiar with the place. 'A beautiful day, isn't it?' he said to the uniformed guard as he climbed the marble stairs.

'Yes, sir,' said the guard.

'Has Major Gleiwitz arrived yet?'

'Just check in with the desk, sir,' said the guard.

'Of course,' said Willi. 'I will. And thank you.' This elicited a smart salute from the guard, which Willi returned.

Willi had an appointment to interview Major Hubert Gleiwitz, a police official and a senior Nazi, about a break-in at his apartment. Frau Bertha Gleiwitz, the major's mother, had been staying with him for the last three weeks since her husband had died. The old lady had been there alone when she walked in on an intruder in the major's bedroom. Her screams had driven the man off.

The major was a genial flatterer and that had endeared him to Hitler and those around him. He loved Hitler, but he loved the intrigue that surrounded him even more. The police department too was rife with intrigue, and the major suspected the break-in was some sort of inside job – inside the Party or the department, he didn't know which. In any case, he wanted the robbery looked into by a disinterested outsider. 'Geismeier's the man,' he told Reineke. 'He doesn't seem capable of intrigue.'

'Are you sure, Major? Geismeier is a thorn in our side,' said Reineke.

'Exactly,' said Gleiwitz. 'I want Geismeier.'

'As you wish, *Herr Major*,' said Reineke.

'Besides, my mother will like him. Send Geismeier to sort this thing out.'

The major told Willi that he thought some Party papers had been taken – 'top-secret planning documents'.

'Was anything else taken, *Herr Major*?'

'Some valuables,' he said with a dismissive wave of his hand.

'I'll need a list of the valuables,' said Willi.

The major offered instead his personal theory as to who might have wanted to break in and what they had to gain from possessing the documents. 'These are documents in the Führer's own hand.'

Willi asked about the valuables again.

'The theft is a diversion, Geismeier. Believe me. I know these men. Look at the Röhm faction, if you want my advice.' Willi let him talk. Each time the major laid out a new theory, he gave away more details about the Party and its inner workings.

'Do you think it could have anything to do with the new SS, *Herr Major*?' Willi said.

'You know I can't talk about that, Geismeier, except to say that the SS, the Schutzstaffel, is Adolf Hitler's highest priority. And there are many people who would like to see it undone. Both within and outside the Party.'

'Can you give me names, *Herr Major*?'

The major named some people he suspected of wanting to undermine the SS project for various reasons, revealing, as he did, rivalries and competing interests within the Gestapo and the Party. 'This is in the strictest confidence, Geismeier.'

'Of course, *Herr Major*,' said Willi. 'You know me. I assume, *Herr Major*, my senior officers – Gruber, Reineke – are beyond suspicion. Otherwise I'd have to take myself off the case.'

'Gruber's a good man,' said the major. 'I have my eyes on him. He's going places.'

'Yes, sir,' said Willi. 'And Captain Reineke.'

The major said nothing.

'May I run some other names by you, *Herr Major*?'

'By all means, Geismeier.'

'Captain Steifflitz,' said Willi. The armory robbery was always in the back of Willi's mind. Other than the two scapegoats, no one had been brought to justice, and the weapons were still out there somewhere.

'Steifflitz? . . . Steifflitz? Can't say that I know him,' said the major.

Willi explained who Steifflitz was.

'Oh, yes. Twenty machine guns, wasn't it? I remember. But that case was closed, wasn't it? That's what Captain Reineke said, if

I recall correctly. Why are you asking about that, Geismeier? Are you trying to ruffle Reineke's feathers again?'

'No, sir, nothing like that, *Herr Major*.' Willi looked at his notes. 'What about Bruck?' he said. 'Otto Bruck?'

The major's face darkened. 'How do you know Dr Bruck?' he said.

'I don't, *Herr Major*. His is a name that came up as a possible witness in a completely different context. I know nothing about him. Do you know him?'

'There's nothing you need to know about him, Geismeier. Stay away from Dr Bruck.'

Gleiwitz looked at his watch. 'Look at the time,' he said and stood up. 'You'll keep me posted, won't you, Geismeier, about the break-in? Mother will be grateful.'

Willi stood up. 'Will you walk me out, *Herr Major*?'

'Of course,' said the major. He wanted to be certain Willi left the building. The two men stopped outside the entrance. The guard stood to attention.

'Thank you, *Herr Major*. This has all been very useful. I'll look in on Frau Gleiwitz tomorrow morning.'

'I'll let her know,' said the major. The two men shook hands and saluted one another.

Wendt, who was watching from a doorway across the street, gave an astonished low whistle. Willi descended the stairs just as a streetcar approached. When the streetcar had passed, he was gone.

The next morning, Bertha Gleiwitz opened the door as soon as Willi rang the bell. She offered him tea but Willi declined. She escorted him through the apartment to the major's bedroom. She showed him where she had first seen the intruder and offered a fairly detailed description of the man's appearance. She did not know him, had never seen him before, but he had made an impression. 'What was it about him that impressed you, Frau Gleiwitz?' Willi said.

'Well, he seemed to know what he was looking for and where to find it. Like he had been here before. He had discovered the secret drawer in Hubert's desk. It was on top of the desk.'

'And what do you think he was he looking for, *gnädige Frau*?' said Willi.

'I only know what he took.'

'And what was that?' said Willi.

She mentioned some silver and some jewelry. She had made a list.

'Did he take any papers, as far as you know?'

'Oh, Hubert is always worried about his secret papers. I don't know anything about that.'

'Could the intruder have been anywhere else in the apartment before you surprised him?'

'Oh, no, Detective,' she said. 'He came in through the bedroom window, and I was in the living room. You have to go through the living room to get from the bedroom to the rest of the apartment, so I would have seen him.'

'And what caused you to go into the bedroom, *gnädige Frau*?'

'I heard a voice.'

'A voice?'

'Yes, Detective. The thief's voice. He was talking.'

'Did you hear anything he said?'

'No.'

'Was it a voice you recognized?'

'No.

'Do you have any idea who he was talking to?'

'Himself, I suppose. He was quite alone when I surprised him.'

'What was he doing when you walked in on him?'

'He was going through my son's desk drawer.'

'The secret one?'

'The center one. He had already gone through the secret one. It was on the desk.'

'Show me which drawer he was going through,' said Willi. She pointed and Willi opened the drawer and looked at it briefly. It contained the major's personal stationery and envelopes, postage stamps, an ink bottle, and other writing supplies.

'And what did he do when you came into the room?' said Willi.

'He leapt through the window. It was still open.'

'And did he say anything before that?'

'Say anything? Detective, we were not having a social afternoon.'

'You said you heard him talking to himself *before* you came in. Did he say anything as he was leaving?'

She thought for a moment. 'Well, yes, you're right. He did. He said, "Watch it," or "Watch out."'

'And then he jumped from the window?'

'Yes.'

'And did you see where he went?'

'No.'

'Now, there's a small garden, then an iron gate, and then an alley down below. Did you hear anything? Someone running, the gate creaking or slamming, a car starting, anything at all?'

'I was expecting to hear something, but I didn't. The gate is rusty and it creaks. And I didn't hear a car start either.'

'And then you called the police?'

'Yes.'

'From the bedroom?'

'No. The phone is in the kitchen.'

'Did you close the window before you left the major's bedroom?'

'You know, I thought I had. But when I went in later it was still open. So I closed it then.'

'You said he took some silver and jewelry. Whose silver and jewelry was it?'

'It was family heirlooms.'

'Just family heirlooms, by which I mean, was any of it *not* family heirlooms?'

She looked through her list. 'No, it was all family heirlooms.'

'And your son kept these family heirlooms in his bedroom? That seems a little unusual to me.'

'Well, it might be. But I had just given them to him the week before. Since my husband died, I wanted to pass them on. He has a safe in the living room. I guess he hadn't had time to put them in the safe, so he had them in a desk drawer.'

'The secret drawer?'

'Not the secret drawer. No.'

'Do you have other children, *gnädige Frau*?'

'I have another son, Detective. But let's not speak of him.'

THE CRIMINAL CLASS

I t turned out Bertha Gleiwitz's second son Hartmut – twelve years younger than the major – was a convicted thief, a repeat offender, recently released from prison, now with a serious drug habit and without a job. He knew of the family heirlooms and that his mother had given them to his brother while he was getting nothing but the back of her hand. 'You'll just sell them,' she'd said.

Hartmut, with the help of a fellow ex-con with housebreaking experience, had decided to help himself to what he thought of as his share of Bertha Gleiwitz's wealth. Hartmut knew she was staying with his brother but had expected her to be out. She usually was at that time of the afternoon. Willi thought they might both have been in the room when she walked in, but that her son was concealed. After she closed the window and left to call the police, Hartmut opened the window again and went out.

Hartmut was arrested and, after a brief interrogation, confessed. 'It's not robbery. That stuff was as much mine as it was his. More, maybe. That shit Nazi prick.' Most of the loot had already disappeared by way of a fence Hartmut had used before. 'I don't have any of it. Neither does Alfred.' Alfred was his partner in crime.

'You don't approve of your brother's politics?' said Willi.

'What? I don't give a shit about his politics. He's an asshole.'

'So, you're not political?'

'Are you crazy?'

'Well, I thought, with your gangster act, you might want to be part of all that. There's lots of money in it, I hear.'

'Yeah, well, they're nuts.'

'You know them?'

'Sure. The joint is full of them.' It finally dawned on Hartmut what Willi was driving at. 'You want to know if I know some of those clowns? Well, I don't. Anyway, I'm not a snitch. Not even for assholes like that.'

'If I told Otto Bruck you and I talked,' said Willi, 'what do you think he'd say?'

'I don't know him,' said Hartmut.

'Listen,' said Willi. 'You can help yourself here . . .'

'You think my mother's going to press charges? You're crazy. She'll be pissed off but I'm still her son. And if she doesn't press charges, then Hubert won't. She's got a lot of money he wants. Momma's boy. It's not going to happen.'

Hartmut was right.

Alfred Streck, Hartmut's partner, was even more reluctant to talk than Hartmut had been. 'You know what happens with snitches?' said Alfred.

'You give me something, and I'll help you,' said Willi.

'Help me? How can you help me?'

'I can do my best to see that you get a fair trial.'

'That doesn't sound like much to me.'

'Listen, Alfred: you robbed an SS major and scared his mother to death. You'll be lucky to get any trial at all. You're going to need all the help you can get just to get in front of a judge, especially a fair judge.'

'Yeah? Well, it was Gleiwitz's idea. He's the mastermind.'

'Really? Well, consider this: Gestapo Major Gleiwitz, your buddy Hartmut's brother, isn't going to press charges against his own flesh and blood. I can guarantee you that. And neither is his mother. But somebody's going down for this, Alfred. You know what that means, don't you? It means you're going to be hung out to dry. No lawyer, no trial. You're on your own here, Alfred.'

Alfred slumped in his chair. Willi offered him a cigarette. 'And you think you can get me a fair trial?'

Willi nodded. 'You give me something useful and I'll do my best.'

'So, what do you want to know?'

'Konrad Milch,' said Willi. 'Ever heard of him?'

Alfred laughed nervously. 'Sure. Everybody has. He's dead, the crazy bastard.'

'Crazy?'

'He scared the shit out of everybody, including his friends.'

'Including you?'

'I didn't know him and didn't want to.'

'So who were his friends?'

Alfred was feeling nervous again. 'That's all I'm giving you.'

'Who were his friends?'

'I can't. Please.'

'These are some bad people, right?'

Alfred remained silent.

'You need friends in high places,' said Willi.

'I've got friends in high places,' said Alfred with a shrug.

'Like Otto Bruck? Maybe I should tell Dr Bruck about the jam you're in. I'm sure he'll want to help.'

'Who's that? I've never heard of him.' Alfred drew deeply on his cigarette, trying to be nonchalant. But his hand trembled, showering ashes onto the table. 'Go ahead,' he said. 'Talk to Bruck. I don't give a shit.'

'Have it your way,' said Willi, gathering his papers and walking out of the room. Alfred stared at the green metal walls, the iron door, the tiny grated window that went nowhere, the lightbulb in the rusty cage on the ceiling. Somebody had carved 'HAHA' into the battered black tabletop in front of him. Alfred rubbed his fingers across the deeply incised letters like a man reading Braille. He took one more drag on his cigarette and crushed it out in the tin can that served as an ashtray. 'Call him back,' he said to the policeman standing by the door.

Willi sat down at the table.

'Don't talk to Bruck about me.'

'OK,' said Willi. 'Milch's friends. Give me names.'

Alfred gave him four names and descriptions. Two of the four sounded like Milch's accomplices that night. Over the next two weeks Willi tracked them down. He found them together one afternoon in a billiard hall. They were standing by a table in the midst of a game when Willi called out their names.

'Who wants to know?' said the one called Jürgen.

'Detective Geismeier,' said Willi. 'Tenth precinct.' Other men who had been standing around watching backed away from the table. *Just like a cowboy movie*, thought Willi. Jürgen and Karl stayed where they were, their cues in their hands, their eyes on the table. Karl was slowly rolling the cue ball back and forth with the flat of his left hand. Back and forth, back and forth. The two men glanced at one another.

The mistake men often made with Willi was to assume from his appearance he would be neither quick nor strong. But as Jürgen lunged, a switchblade in his hand, Willi slid sideways, grabbed a pool cue by the wrong end, and, swinging it like a bat, caught Jürgen full in the side. You could hear his ribs break as he crumpled to the ground. Karl took a step toward Willi. Willi pulled a pistol out of the holster at the small of his back, and Karl thought better of it.

Willi guarded the two men – Karl face down, his hands cuffed behind him, and Jürgen moaning nearby – until three patrolmen arrived to take Karl to jail and Jürgen to the hospital. Both men had served time and were wanted on outstanding warrants, which was why Bruck had had to find stand-ins for them as witnesses to Milch's death.

Jürgen and Karl both professed allegiance to Hitler, but neither man knew much about Hitler's program or, for that matter, had any serious interest in it. They liked the patriotism stuff, the idea of getting rid of foreigners, and the street fighting. Their anti-Semitism was just as casual. Karl's grandmother was a Jew. 'She was a nasty old bitch,' said Karl. 'So to hell with her and her kike tribe.'

The NSDAP represented a golden opportunity; it was an irresistible expression of their anarchic soul. Both men were devoted thieves, and the Party practically invited them to rob and sow mayhem with impunity. Who knew whether it would last? But as long as it did, and their mayhem advanced the cause, why would they want to be anywhere else?

Karl mostly stayed in an apartment in the city. But sometimes, when he needed to disappear, he stayed with his mother, an occasional prostitute, who lived in a hut beside the train tracks by Krailling. She was frightened of Karl; he beat her up sometimes. 'Just like his father,' she said.

She lived in an alcoholic fog now, but, yes, she said, she knew Jürgen. 'His mother used to be a friend of mine, before . . .' Her voice trailed off. 'Jürgen and Karl played together back then. He was sweet.' She brushed the hair back from her face, and that one gesture told Willi everything about her hardship, longing, and sadness. She recalled another 'friend' of Karl's, an older man with a black hand. 'Very nice,' she said. 'But he didn't come back.'

'When did you last see that man here?' said Willi.

'Oh, it's been years,' she said.

'Does the shack back in the woods belong to you?'

'I used to keep chickens,' she said. 'Not anymore.'

The shack had a rusted corrugated roof and sides of rotting wood. Vines of ivy and honeysuckle had climbed up and over the walls and door. Willi pulled at the door; it wouldn't open. When Willi pulled again, a little harder this time, the screws holding the hinges tore out of the rotten wood. Another tug or two and the whole shack might have come down.

Willi squeezed through the door. The inside was covered with vines too. It smelled of the mice and rats that lived there now. Someone had laid down some boards as a makeshift floor, and in a hole in the earth under the boards was a large canvas bundle tied up with rope. It contained a substantial cache of military weapons. The serial numbers had been mostly filed off. But when Willi came back with the list of weapons stolen from the armory, there was enough of a match to identify these as those weapons. There were also some metal boxes containing some cash, but mostly miscellaneous goods, obviously robbery loot: jewelry, dinnerware, silverware, candlesticks. One small box contained nothing but pocket watches. Willi puzzled over the pocket watches for a while. He took them with him when he left.

Karl's lawyer, a ferret-eyed martinet named Stefan Müller, smirked in Willi's direction as Willi entered the interrogation room. Willi took a watch out of his pocket and laid it open on the table. He opened the file he had put together on Karl and studied it for a moment. 'I see, Karl, that you have had an interesting and long career. Long for such a young man. Your mother tells me' – Karl's eyes narrowed, he looked at Müller and then back at Willi – 'your mother says that you have been a thief pretty much your entire life.'

Karl remained silent, his face blank.

'You seem to specialize in watches.'

Karl looked bored.

'I'm guessing that you see a watch and you almost can't resist taking it. Herr Müller, you may want to check your pocket, to see whether you still have yours. Am I right, Karl?'

'Listen, Detective,' said the lawyer, 'I'm sure you find this amusing. But I assure you that my client – who, by the way, has a family name, which is Meier, which both he and I would like you to use – my client, Herr Meier, and I find it both tedious and extremely un-amusing. Herr Meier has been charged with theft of government property and assault, and we would like to hear of any evidence you have that backs up these charges.'

Willi presented the evidence that Karl was involved in the armory theft – the weapons in his mother's shed.

'His *mother* was in possession of those weapons,' said Müller.

'Not Herr Meier.'

'The testimony of other witnesses,' said Willi.

'What witnesses?' said Müller.

'His mother will testify that Karl and his friend Jürgen brought the weapons and hid them in her shed.'

'You're relying,' said Müller, 'on the word of a drunken whore. And the other witnesses?'

Willi remained silent.

'I thought so,' said Müller. 'I presume the assault charge is just as flimsy.'

'He assaulted a police officer . . .'

'He didn't touch you, Detective.'

'And his part in the death of Konrad Milch,' said Willi.

Karl had been gazing at the watch on the table. Now he looked up. 'What are you talking about?' said Müller.

'Milch, Jurgen, and Karl entered the English Garden around midnight on the night of Friday, December 14, 1923 with assault on their mind. They attacked a couple – an artist and a journalist – with a lead pipe, with the clear intent of killing them. They had a pistol as well as the pipe. When Milch was shot dead, they ran. Come on, Karl. You haven't even told your own lawyer what happened?'

Karl started to speak, but Müller silenced him. 'And you have evidence of this?'

'The two intended victims and a third bystander.'

'And what are the names of these so-called victims?'

'Ask Karl,' said Willi. 'Oh, sorry: ask Herr Meier.'

GOOD TIMES

One evening, as 1924 was coming to an end, Willi went to one of the Horvaths' gatherings. He arrived a little early. The Horvaths seemed in good health, although Benno was frailer now and more circumspect than when Willi had seen him last. He embraced Willi with urgency. 'How are you?' said Benno, holding Willi by the shoulders. 'Are you all right?'

'Have you heard something?' Willi said.

Benno shrugged. 'I don't hear much any more, but I still know a couple of people. They know you are interested in Otto Bruck. So he knows it too. I don't have to tell you, he is extremely dangerous.'

'Do you know him?' said Willi.

'I know of him.'

'He's a school principal,' said Willi.

'Now he is. Before that he was a medical doctor. Under a different name. I'll get it for you.'

'So, who is he really?'

'I don't know, but whoever else he is, he's a criminal. And he's been a devotee of Hitler's since the beginning. Thanks to his ruthlessness, he's become one of Hitler's favorites. He and Röhm have been keeping the Party in shape while Hitler's in prison. And they know about you.'

'I met him once, briefly,' said Willi.

The doorbell rang.

'Be careful, Willi,' said Benno, placing a hand against Willi's cheek. 'I can't protect you.'

The Swedish diplomat Edvin Lindstrom came into the room. *Geheimrat* Gerhardt Riegelmann arrived a moment later. He and Lindstrom avoided one another except for a handshake and a perfunctory *guten Abend*.

Gottfried Büchner, the film critic, was there and in an ebullient frame of mind. After the guests were sitting here and there, Büchner opined that things were looking up for Germany. The central government had managed to stabilize the currency by issuing new money and tying its worth to the wealth of the nation.

'But not before people's savings disappeared into thin air,' someone else said, obviously speaking about themselves.

'Well, at least, the inflation is over,' said someone else. It had gone as high as fifty billion German marks to the dollar, which meant the mark was worthless. People had stories about running to cash their paycheck and spending the money immediately on whatever groceries it could buy before its value fell further. People used suitcases or wheelbarrows to carry cash.

'I had a neighbor who was robbed,' said Büchner. 'The robbers dumped out the money and ran off with his wheelbarrow.' Everyone started laughing and then couldn't stop.

'Thank God that's behind us,' said Margarete finally when everyone had caught their breath.

The burden of the war reparations had also been eased, thanks to the Dawes Plan, which Riegelmann tried to explain, but, when it came down to it, no one could quite understand. It had to do with the removal of occupation troops from the Ruhr area, the staggering of reparation payments, and other economic manipulations. Anyway, it seemed to be helping facilitate a vigorous reconciliation with the Allies and, miracle of miracles, a growing economy.

'I have to say,' said Margarete, 'shopping is a pleasure again. There are things to buy. That probably sounds frivolous.'

'No, no, not at all, my dear,' said Benno, and everyone else chimed in.

The cold roast beef was plentiful and delicious. There was French champagne.

'The Republic is up in the polls. Even Stresemann is popular,' said Riegelmann. He did not seem happy about it.

'Well, it's thanks to stability,' said Oscar Sponeck, an investment banker. 'Everybody wants stability, and the government that ushers it in, whether it's their accomplishment or not, will always be rewarded.'

'Well, Stresemann accomplished nothing,' said Riegelmann. 'Either as Chancellor or as Foreign Minister. Nothing.'

'Maybe not,' said Sponeck. 'But it doesn't really matter. What matters is who's in office when it happens. It happened on Stresemann's watch, so he gets the credit. I think 1925 is going to be a very good year.'

'To Germany's future,' said Büchner, lifting his flute of champagne. Everyone else raised their glasses in agreement. 'By the way, what's happened to the Nazis?' said Sponeck. 'You don't hear much about them anymore, do you?'

'Hitler's in jail, and they're saying they're done for,' said a young woman. 'And good riddance.' No one there had a kind word to say about Hitler or his National Socialist German Workers' Party anymore.

Not long after that, Willi found himself in Edvin Lindstrom's small, spare office at the Swedish Consulate. Edvin had invited him for tea. 'Have you been to Japan?' Willi asked. He stood studying one of the Japanese prints Lindstrom had hung facing the window.

Lindstrom had been to Japan, although he had never served there. 'Not yet anyway,' he said. 'I admire the culture, though, and would like to be posted there some day.'

The two men sat in silence for a while and sipped their tea. Finally Willi wondered aloud how Lindstrom's opinions about Germany might have changed since that first time they had met.

'That was a while ago, wasn't it?' said Lindstrom. 'The Horvaths are such lovely people. I didn't want to cast gloom over their recent soiree.'

'Which means, I take it,' said Willi, 'that there's gloom to be cast?'

'Well, you know, Willi, we Scandinavians are a gloomy people,' said Edvin.

'So, everything's fine?' said Willi.

Edvin smiled. 'Not exactly. At least not in my opinion,' he said. 'Hitler's trial, for instance. It changed everything, and not necessarily for the better.'

'At least it took him off the public stage,' said Willi. 'No one talks about him anymore, unless it's as a joke.'

'And that's a big mistake,' said Edvin.

'You think so?' said Willi.

'Did you follow the trial at all?'

'Not really. Did you?'

'Yes, I did,' said Edvin. 'I followed it closely; I was there for most of it. I expect he'll be released from prison soon.'

'Really?' said Willi. 'But the trial was just last spring. The sentence was five years, wasn't it?'

'It was. But with parole possible after eight months.'

'And?'

'It's been over eight months. I expect he'll be paroled.'

'Really?'

'From what I hear, he's been a model prisoner,' said Edvin. 'His guards and wardens treat him like royalty. He's gotten fat from all the cakes and cheeses people bring him.'

'And what do you make of all that?' said Willi.

'I think we're living in the calm before the storm,' Edvin said. 'Sure, Germany's having a good moment. But I don't think that's going to last. The economic boom is built on quicksand, on the illusion that there's bedrock supporting this new prosperity. But German prosperity is built mostly on American money, and that won't last forever. And the Dawes Plan, which has relaxed reparations and other unpopular aspects of the Versailles Treaty, is unlikely to solve anything. Allowing Germany to rearm, for instance, in light of the ongoing political instability, is extremely dangerous.

'I hope you don't take this personally, Willi. But you Germans are all in favor of democracy when times are good and prosperity is on the rise. But when things go bad, you don't have the patience for it. Meanwhile, you still have a very divided country. The upper classes are on one side of things, the poor and discontented are on the other. And everyone, whatever side they're on, is just looking for a savior, some hero to shake things up and magically build a new, better society.

'Did you know that while Hitler's been in prison he's had a constant stream of visitors? Pilgrims have been going to Landsberg to pay homage. I heard he asked them to stop coming. You know why? He's writing a book. I haven't heard exactly what it's about. But it's easy to guess. It will be all about him, a grandiose memoir, probably laying out his plans to lead Germany back to greatness.'

Hitler was released from prison four days before Christmas. He was escorted to the arched iron gate by the warden, who then took his hand in both of his and pumped it warmly. Guards lined up to say their farewells as well. Hitler was followed by his disciples carrying his papers and personal belongings to a waiting car.

'*Ein feiner Mann*,' said the warden as they drove off.

They sped through the wintery landscape. The snow shimmered under a wintery sun. They passed through Windach and Greifenberg and Inning am Ammersee. They were passing a lake, the Wörthsee, when Hitler said to stop. He got out and walked to the frozen lake's edge. He stared across the snow-covered ice. 'That island,' he said pointing. 'Mouse Island. You know why they call it that?' Of course no one knew.

'An old legend,' he said. 'A terrible famine. The count was asked for food by his starving peasants. The count had the peasants driven into a barn. He set the barn on fire. When the cries of the peasants had finally stopped, the count heard another noise, a kind of faint whimpering. "What's that?" he said. "That, *mein Herr*, is the mice and rats who are also suffering."

'"Well," said the count, "exterminate them as well," and climbed onto his horse and rode back to his castle. One evening, as the count was being served dinner, the dining hall filled suddenly with rats and mice who swarmed onto the table and ate the food from his plate and from all the platters and serving bowls. The count fled by horse and then by boat, to that island. But the mice and rats followed him there, where they ate him alive.' Then, without saying another word, he got in the car and they drove off. His men puzzled all the way to Munich over the meaning in this bizarre parable.

The city was decorated for Christmas with greenery and colored lights. The streets were bustling with holiday shoppers. Hitler took little notice. He had had eight months to think and plan and reconsider, and now his future, Germany's future – they were one and the same – was all he could think about.

Hitler's followers were more eager than ever for an armed insurrection. They felt the revolution slipping away from them but were convinced it could succeed this time. They thought they now had the army on their side, and the Berlin government, they said, was increasingly despised. This was the moment to act.

'No,' said Hitler. 'Insurrection is not the way. The Putsch was a mistake. We have to hold our noses and run for office. We have to be elected to the Reichstag; we have to run and win against the Socialist and Catholic and Marxist deputies. That's the only way we will come to power.

'Outvoting them may take longer than outshooting them. But when they are finally outvoted – and they *will* be outvoted – the result will be guaranteed by their own ridiculous democracy. Our victory will be completely legitimate according to their law. They will be bound by their democratic principles to uphold our duly elected dictatorship. 'Yes, I know what you're going to say. The process is too slow. And you're right: it is slow. But before long we will have a majority, and then we will have Germany. Germany will be ours.'

Their first task, he said, was to rebuild the National Socialist German Workers' Party from the ground up. They had to transform the Party from the diminishing collection of fractious malcontents and misfits into a smoothly functioning political machine. To accomplish that they had to stop all the backbiting and feuding among factions. 'And the only way to do that is to place the Party under my absolute control.' The NSDAP would be an extension of the Leader, *der Führer* – as he had begun to call himself – from whom all order and meaning would flow.

Hitler said all this to a roomful of his most devoted followers, men who had been with him through thick and thin. 'Our movement must be irresistible, unstoppable,' he said. 'And it must be organized as though it were already the government that it will eventually become.' The men all looked at one another.

'But, *mein Führer*,' said someone, 'the setbacks . . .'

'The setbacks are insignificant. Less than insignificant! They are nothing.' He gave a dismissive wave of his hand. 'This government of traitors in Berlin is a pitiful cripple, propped up by American money. And, never forget: the German people's humiliation isn't going away; it sticks in our throats like a chicken bone. Every true German has a yearning, an insatiable thirst for vengeance and victory. And we will bring that to them.'

'But, *mein Führer*, look at the recent elections. The socialists are gaining . . .'

'Stop it!' he shouted. 'Stop it!' He jumped up and leaned forward, his fists on the table. 'Not another word, do you hear me?' His voice rose to a shriek. 'I will not tolerate doubt and defeatism. Is that understood?' His fists were clenched, his eyes were wide, his mouth was a hard, grey line. He stared hard from one man to the next. They remained silent.

'Now here are your posts,' he said. The storm had passed. He nodded to Rudolf Hess, who handed around a list with their names attached to various offices and departments: treasury, defense, foreign affairs, domestic affairs, industry, agriculture, race and culture, propaganda. These were to be ministries in the coming NSDAP government, he said. 'And you are my ministers.' The men looked at one another, then found their names on the list. They were astonished.

Hitler unrolled a map, and the men got up from their chairs and crowded around the table. He had drawn red lines dividing the country into political districts he called *Gaue*. He had given each district an old Germanic name like *Ostmark, Schlesien, Sachsen, Pommern*, and begun selecting a *Gauleiter* – district leader – for each. Each district would in turn contain multiple circles or *Kreise*, with their own dedicated leader or *Kreisleiter*. And each circle would contain local groups with group leaders. And each group leader would have sworn allegiance not to Germany but to the Führer. 'We will be organized down to every village, every city block. Everything will be in place when the time comes. As it will.'

Even though the Party had been forbidden in Bavaria and throughout Germany, and the number of its adherents had shrunk to national insignificance, Hitler saw himself ruling Germany as though dominance by the NSDAP were an unassailable and inevitable fact. His genius was that he made the men gathered around him see it too.

Hitler made an appointment to meet Heinrich Held, the newly elected Bavarian State President, the man who could lift the ban against the Party. Held was an elderly and congenial man, a Catholic conservative, an orderly man whose political agenda centered around peace and conciliation.

'Herr Hitler,' announced the president's secretary as he showed Hitler into the office. The president looked up but remained seated. He put on an unsmiling face. Instead of the swaggering, blustering demagogue he had expected, however, he saw a diffident man, dressed in a suit and overcoat, with his hat in his hand. Hitler bowed slightly.

'*Herr Präsident*,' said Hitler and took the president's hand in his and bowed again. 'Thank you for seeing me.' Held invited Hitler to sit and they spoke for a half-hour. The president was stern at first. He said the Bavarian government would under no circumstances put up with the outrageous behavior in Hitler's past, and would use the entire authority and force of the state to prevent it happening again.

Hitler looked down at his hands. '*Herr Präsident*,' he said finally, 'I cannot express how deeply sorry I am for much of my past behavior, most particularly for the attempted coup d'état. That was a terrible error for which I have been justifiably punished. I believe in the supremacy of the law and of the elected government, of *your* government, and I promise my allegiance to it. I promise too that I will do everything to make amends for my past behavior.' His expressions of remorse went on for some time. President Held found them fulsome and convincing. He saw that he was dealing with a changed man.

The prohibition against both the NSDAP and Hitler's public speaking were soon lifted. 'The beast is tamed,' President Held said. 'We can loosen the shackles.'

'The man is a fool and an idiot,' said Hitler.

THE GOOD COP

Penzigauerstraße was a street Bergemann had never heard of. It was in a neighborhood made up mostly of industrial buildings that had emptied out after the war and then fallen into neglect and ruin. Many were boarded up or had broken windows. No buses or streetcars came anywhere nearby. A few people lived here and there, but most were squatting illegally. The red-brick building, number twenty-six, looked like it might have once been a factory or warehouse, something other than the apartment block it seemed to have become.

Detective Bergemann had to catch his breath after climbing three flights of stairs. He thought maybe it was nerves. He knocked on the door, tugged at his jacket, and smoothed his hair. A woman opened the door. 'Good morning,' he said. 'I'm looking for Willi Geismeier.'

'Who are you?' she said. She had a foreign accent.

'Detective Hans Bergemann. I'm a colleague . . . a former colleague of Detective Geismeier.'

'Just a minute,' she said and closed the door. He heard footsteps on the stairs behind him as a man passed on his way downstairs. He gave Bergemann a hard look up and down. Bergemann was in plain clothes, but he still looked like a cop. Finally the door opened.

'Hello, Herr Geismeier,' said Bergemann and held out his hand.

Willi took it. 'Hello, Bergemann.' They hadn't seen each other for over a year.

'How are you, Herr Geismeier? I would have called first, but no one has your phone number and it's not listed.'

'No,' said Willi. 'But you found my address.'

'Well,' Bergemann smiled sheepishly, 'I'm a detective.'

'What do you want?' said Willi.

'I need your help.'

'Do you?' said Willi. He didn't sound interested, and gave no indication he was going to invite Bergemann inside.

'Could we talk somewhere private?'

'Just a minute,' said Willi and closed the door. Bergemann waited.

He began to wonder whether that was the end of their conversation when the door opened again and Willi came out wearing an overcoat.

'It's warming up; the sun is out,' said Bergemann. *Why did I say that?* he wondered.

Willi led the way down the stairs to the street. Bergemann wondered whether Willi was paying rent or squatting. Was the woman at the door his wife?

Willi and Bergemann walked four blocks to a small cafe with no name or sign. They were the only customers. Willi took off his coat, hung it on a hook, and then sat down at the nearest table. 'What'll you have, Bergemann?'

'*Ein kleines bier,*' said Bergemann. Willi held up two fingers to the man at the bar, who poured off two beers. They lifted their two glasses toward one another without a word.

'I wanted to talk to you about the Otto Bruck case,' said Bergemann finally. He wiped the foam from his mustache with the back of his finger.

'Who is Otto Bruck?' said Willi.

'When they suspended you, I went through your desk. I found your notes.'

'And there was something there about an Otto Bruck?'

'He's the one that got you suspended, isn't he?'

'Is he?' said Willi.

'And that happened right after the two goons with Milch got indicted. What were their names?'

'Listen, Bergemann. You show up out of the blue one fine day when, as you say, "the sun is out," and imagine you can get me to tell you what I know and don't know. I'm not a cop anymore, but I'm not an idiot. I don't know what you're up to. But if you don't stop playing this stupid fishing game immediately, our little visit is over.'

Bergemann looked stunned. 'OK,' he said after a moment. 'Fair enough.' He cracked his knuckles. He rubbed his cheeks and his chin, as though he might be searching for a different approach to a difficult story. 'OK,' he said again. 'I overheard Gruber and Reineke talking about Otto Bruck. It was the day you were fired . . . suspended. And I guessed you were getting close to something or they wouldn't have suspended you. So I went backwards through the calendar and came upon' – he pulled a notepad from his pocket

and read – 'Karl Meier and Jürgen Veit. You arrested them and
interviewed them at length. There were no interview notes, which
was odd. And there were letters of complaint from their lawyer'
– he read his notes again – 'Stefan Müller. Letters that gave me
his version of the interviews. He didn't mention Bruck by name,
but he talked about an "injured party". Müller works for Bruck.
So I figured that's who he was referring to. I started looking into
Bruck a little.' Bergemann looked at Willi, waiting for him to say
something, but Willi remained silent.

Bergemann continued, 'Bruck's employed as a school superin-
tendent. But he's been suspected of various crimes, some quite
serious, that he is supposed to have committed using different
names. He has friends in high places, so he has rarely been formally
charged and has never been convicted of anything. The couple of
times he *has* been charged, the judge ruled that the evidence was
insufficient, even though the evidence looks substantial to me, and
so the cases never came to trial.'

'Insufficient?' said Willi.

'Well, he's been associated with people who turned up dead.
In fact, judging from his connections, activities, and whereabouts
back then, I think he was probably involved in' – the notebook
again – 'the February 21, 1919 assassination of the Bavarian
Premier, Kurt Eisner. I also think he may have been involved in
blowing up the *Bild* newspaper offices where the editor was
killed. You were on that case, as I recall. So, yes, I think there's
a Bruck case.'

Willi gave Bergemann a long look. 'It doesn't sound like you
need any help from me.'

'Here's the thing, Herr Geismeier . . . Willi. Gruber's getting
big-time pressure from on high – Reineke and probably even
higher. As I say, Bruck's got high-up friends, and somebody thinks
you're still on Bruck's case.'

'I'm not,' said Willi. 'How could I be? I'm suspended.'

'They think you're still investigating, and they want you
stopped.'

'And you came to warn me?'

Bergemann laughed. 'Well, yes and no. I did want to warn you,
but I mainly came because Gruber told me to. To find out what
you're up to, what you know.'

'So, what are you going to tell him?'

'I don't know exactly. I have to tell him something. I'd love it if you could throw me a bone, some harmless bit of news, that would get him off your case. And maybe off mine too.'

'Some harmless bit of news.'

'Gruber's caught in a bind. He thought being a Nazi would be fun, that he could use Nazis – like Reineke – to get ahead. Now it's turning out otherwise. Reineke doesn't trust Gruber anymore. Turns out his wife's a Jew, so Gruber missed out on getting in the SS. He's probably never going higher than detective sergeant, and he knows it. Even Wendt has been promoted over him.'

'Robert Wendt, your old partner?'

'Yeah, well. We took different paths, Robert and I.'

'Aha.'

'I know you'll think I'm bullshitting you, Willi, but I have to say this anyway: I owe you a lot. There was a moment not too long ago – you were already gone – when I decided to be a good cop. It was when I realized what a bad cop I had been. Lazy, indifferent, oblivious. I admit it. Going along to get along. I know – everybody knows – that you're a good cop. Even Gruber and Reineke and Wendt and the others know it. So, once I decided to change my ways, I looked to you to see what exactly being a good cop would mean.'

He paused. Willi said nothing. Bergemann went on. 'I also looked at you to see what mistakes you made that I could avoid. Do you want to hear this?'

'I'm listening,' said Willi.

'I think your most serious mistake was your unwillingness to make compromises, to be sociable. You never went to departmental parties, never went for a beer with your colleagues after your shift. You weren't friendly.'

'I'm still not,' said Willi.

Bergemann laughed. 'You seemed to go out of your way to do stuff to annoy people. You rubbed them the wrong way. It looked like you did it on purpose.'

'Maybe I did.'

'Well, the way I see it, you have to make small compromises so you don't have to make big ones. For instance, the police and the SA still feud sometimes, but they're coming together. They'll merge before long. So I wear the SA uniform sometimes now. I know you'd never do that. But it turns out it's an effective disguise.

Nobody sees you when you're in uniform. They see a storm trooper, and I remain invisible. Sociability, compromise, those can be disguises too.'

Willi drank his last sip of beer, set the glass down and turned it, making a wet circle on the coaster. Bergemann couldn't tell what Willi might be thinking or whether he was thinking at all. Finally, though, after a long silence, Willi looked up and said, 'I *do* have something for you, Bergemann. But it's far from harmless.'

'What is it?'

'I'll send it to you,' said Willi.

'You could give it to me.'

'I'll send it to you.'

On Friday afternoon, Bergemann got an envelope. There was no return address. It had been hand delivered; the desk officer couldn't say by whom. Inside was a letter and, attached with a paper clip, the drawn likenesses of Konrad Milch and Otto Bruck.

> *Detective Hans Bergemann,*
>
> *Walther Hinzig, a pressman at the newspaper,* Das Neue Deutsche Bild, *was an eyewitness to the bombing of the newspaper offices in which Erwin Czieslow was killed. Herr Hinzig described both of the bombers to an artist who drew these likenesses from his descriptions. No one in the department knows of the existence of these drawings.*
>
> *This information is being delivered to the* Munich Post *and to the Bavarian state prosecutor at the same time it is being sent to you.*

There followed a brief list of other forensic evidence that had been collected after the bombing that could be found in the department Evidence Room, unless it had been removed. Bergemann copied out the list of forensic evidence for his own use, then took everything to Gruber. Gruber read the letter and looked at the drawings. He reread the letter. 'Jesus. Which prosecutor? There are twenty prosecutors in that office.'

'Eighteen,' said Bergemann.

'OK, eighteen,' said Gruber. 'So, which prosecutor?'

'He didn't say,' said Bergemann. 'He didn't tell me this was coming.'

'And he didn't say anything about giving this to the *Post*?'

'Nothing.'

'What did you find out about his life these days? Is he still working?'

'He said no. But then this' – he pointed to the letter – 'says otherwise.'

'What else?'

'He lives at Penzigauerstraße 26, third floor, apartment B. There's a woman.'

'His wife?'

'I couldn't say.' Bergemann anticipated the next question. 'He didn't let me inside.'

'Jesus Christ, Bergemann. All you managed to do was warn him we're onto him.'

'He knew that already. I told you . . .'

'I know, I know,' said Gruber. 'Go see that reporter woman. Sophie whatshername. Threaten her a little. Find out what the *Post* is doing with this stuff.'

Bergemann went to the *Post* as instructed. Security guards at the entrance checked his identification. The receptionist opened the office directory to Sophie's name. 'I'm sorry, sir, she's not in the office.'

'When will she be back?'

'Oh, not for some time. She's away.'

'She still works for the *Post*, doesn't she?'

'Yes, sir. But she's on leave.'

'On leave?'

'Maternity leave,' said the receptionist flashing a happy smile. 'She's having a baby!'

SUSPENSION

Otto Bruck knew he couldn't just kill Willi. You kill a Munich cop, even an asshole like Willi Geismeier, and the entire police force will rise up against you. Otto had pulled strings behind the scenes to get Willi fired for insubordination, thinking that then he could deal with him as he wanted to. And he had almost succeeded. After all, insubordination was ridiculously easy to prove when it came to Detective Geismeier. Between them, Gruber and Reineke had page after page of instances. But Willi, it turned out, also had friends in high places. So an indefinite suspension was the best Bruck and his friends could manage.

There was no trial, but Willi was entitled to a formal suspension ceremony, and for some reason he wanted that. The ceremony took place in Reineke's office. Willi was not in uniform, but he had pinned all his commendation ribbons to his rumpled suit jacket. Reineke read aloud instance after instance of misbehavior, getting angrier and angrier as he read. Then he announced that Detective Willi Geismeier was herewith suspended from the Munich police force until further notice while his case was reviewed.

Willi stood at attention. 'Goddamn it, Geismeier,' said Reineke when he was finished, 'I hope you're satisfied. You've undermined investigation after investigation, interfered with others, and in the process ruined your own career, what could have been a perfectly good police career. What do you have to say for yourself?'

'Will that be all, Captain?' said Willi.

'What?' said Reineke. He needed to be sure due process was followed, and Geismeier wasn't even going to make *that* easy. More than a few higher-ups were in the room, Major Gleiwitz among them, who had not at all been on board with Willi's suspension. Yes, he freely admitted, Detective Geismeier was difficult. He had unconventional methods, and he flouted regulations. But he was a skillful investigator and he still cleared far more cases than other detectives. 'I mean, look at him: he has more decorations than all the other detectives, and most of his superiors as well.'

'You have the right to speak, Detective Geismeier,' said Reineke, one eye on Major Gleiwitz. 'You are guaranteed the right to speak.'

'Will that be all, Captain?' said Willi again.

'All right, Geismeier. Have it your way.' He snapped to attention. 'Dismissed!' he said, his voice trembling with rage.

Willi saluted, did an about face, and walked out of the office.

'I warned you about Bruck,' said Major Gleiwitz later, when he and Willi were together. 'You should never have messed with that man.'

'Yes, sir, you warned me,' said Willi.

'This could cost you your career. Is it worth it?'

'Time will tell, sir. It's out of my hands now.'

'What have you got on Bruck anyway, Geismeier?'

Willi remained silent.

'OK, fine, I understand. But, whatever it is, it's somebody else's case now.'

Again Willi said nothing.

'You've done a lot of good police work, Geismeier. And you did a damn fine job for my mother, and my goddamn idiot brother. She thanks you, and I thank you. My brother should thank you too, but that's another story.' The two men shook hands.

So Willi Geismeier was gone. Or was he? Otto Bruck hadn't counted on the loyalty of cops to one another. Even those who didn't like Willi didn't like seeing him screwed over for political reasons, and that was plainly what had just gone on. In this new political police force, this sort of thing was happening more and more. Every cop imagined he could be the next one it happened to. Willi Geismeier may have been a jerk, but at least he was *their* jerk.

Otto Bruck learned about the drawing of him from one of the Bavarian state prosecutors. When he saw it he was startled by the likeness. 'That's me, all right. Jesus. What happens now?'

'It's too late to bury it,' said the prosecutor. 'An investigating judge will look at it and decide whether to bring charges. But even if they do, this doesn't prove anything. It's not something I'd worry too much about.'

Stefan Müller, Otto's lawyer, said the same thing. 'Don't worry. It's a drawing by someone who wasn't there, made from a description by an addled old man. As a piece of evidence, it's useless. As long as there isn't other corroborating evidence.'

When the *Post* took a look at everything they had on Bruck and the bombing, their editors and lawyers came to the same conclusion, albeit reluctantly. 'Bruck's a murderous swine; we know that. But we need more before this is a story.' And the investigating judge reacted similarly. 'It's not enough to build a case on,' he said.

'I think Geismeier's tipped his hand,' said Stefan Müller. 'He can't have anything else, or it would have come out now.'

Otto gave Müller a look that caused him to pause.

'Can he?' said Müller.

'Don't be ridiculous,' said Bruck, waving the question aside. Something else had just occurred to him. 'He must have had this drawing for years, right?'

'Yes. Since right after the bombing, I would think.'

'So why now? Why hold on to it all this time and then release it now?'

'Because he's scared of you now,' said Müller. 'You got him suspended. He's afraid of what's next.'

'No, no, that's not it. There's something else. Something's missing here.'

'Maybe he kept it as a kind of ace in the hole.'

'But why release it now, at this moment? Maybe he was protecting someone by not releasing the picture.'

'Besides himself?' said Müller. 'Who?'

'That's the question, isn't it? Who's he protecting?' said Otto.

'You figure that out,' said Müller, 'and we've got him.'

MARIA CHRISTINE

Maria Christine Wolf was born just after midnight. It was a warm night, the second day of June 1929, and she lay in a large painted bed that looked more like a sleigh than a bed, in a farmhouse in Bad Stauffenheim, a farming village two hours southeast of Munich. The birth went smoothly. Maria Christine was pink and plump and in full voice. Sophie was exhausted and happy.

Maximilian and his parents, August and Ingeborg Wolf, whose house it was, were in the room. The room and its furnishings, not just the bed, were brightly painted as was often the case in farmhouses in upper Bavaria. The ceiling beams and supporting posts were entwined with painted garlands of red, blue, and yellow flowers. Red-cheeked peasants in costumes and jolly birds and animals danced across the doors, up and down the giant armoire, and across the shutters framing the windows.

Sophie had been certain she would never bring children into this world, until it had dawned on her that the arduous and dangerous work she had been doing had been dedicated to a future generation that existed only in her imagination. Maximilian was delighted when Sophie said she wanted a child, because, he said, he was a child himself, and now he would have someone to play with. Although neither Sophie nor Maximilian believed in God, they gave their child a name that sounded, each time you said it, like a small prayer of hope and celebration, an incantation, affirmation of something they knew was not there, but might, through some miracle, come into being. They never gave her a nickname; they never called her anything but Maria Christine.

The plan was that Sophie and Maria Christine would stay in Bad Stauffenheim for the summer. Maximilian would come for long weekends. He was busy with Aaron Appelbaum putting together a show of drawings and small paintings for the London gallery. 'If this is successful,' said Aaron, 'then next year we'll try New York.'

* * *

Two uniformed policemen showed up at the *Post* asking to see Sophie Auerbach. They were told she was away. They asked where she was. The receptionist explained that she was on leave. They asked again where she was. When the receptionist declined to tell them, they demanded to speak with the editor.

Franz Ortner, the editor, asked why they needed that information. They said they had a warrant for Sophie Auerbach's arrest and that Ortner had a legal obligation to give them her address. He gave them the address in Bad Stauffenheim. As soon as the policemen left, Ortner called Sophie to let her know that the police were coming. It took a while for the call to go through.

Meanwhile, his assistant tracked down Maximilian. Maximilian ran to the station as soon as he heard and took the next train to Salzburg. He was glad he had a compartment to himself; he did not want to share his terror with strangers. He gazed from the window as the city seemed to trickle away. Large buildings gave way to smaller ones which gave way to open space and trees heavy with new leaves. Telephone lines swooped past, roads converged and then darted away. The yellow wheat fields turned suddenly to green peas or alfalfa and then back again or to cows or to a village, snow-covered mountains in the distance. The world moved past, shifting this way and that, filled with indecipherable meaning, like a sped-up life, like silent music.

He woke up when the compartment door slid open and the conductor and border official came in. The train was moving slowly. They were coming into Salzburg. The train stopped with a lurch and a mighty sigh. The bus to Bad Stauffenheim was waiting on the square out front.

In Bad Stauffenheim Maximilian ran from the stop by the Hotel zum Post to his parents' house, but he was too late. His mother held Maria Christine, tiny and oblivious to everything. Maximilian took the baby and kissed her again and again.

Two police officers escorted Sophie back to Munich. They were respectful. They helped her in and out of the car. One of them asked about the baby. 'How old?'

'Eight weeks,' said Sophie.

'I've got a one-year-old,' he said.

In Munich she was taken directly to the courthouse. She sat between the two policemen and waited. They didn't talk any more. After an hour or so a man hurried toward them and introduced himself as her attorney. 'Robert Fitzmorris,' he said. 'My father was a Scot.' His name was everyone's first question, so he always answered before they asked. Fitzmorris wanted a little time alone with his client, and the two policemen moved to chairs across the hall.

Finally – it was after six – the four of them were escorted into a small courtroom where the charge was read: second-degree murder for shooting Konrad Milch to death.

The prosecutor, a fat, balding man with thick glasses and a small mustache, asked that Sophie be held without bail because of the seriousness of the crime. Robert Fitzmorris argued that Sophie had an infant daughter who was nursing and needed her mother. Moreover, she lived in Munich, where she was gainfully employed as a newspaper reporter, and, thus, posed no flight risk. Besides, she was innocent of the charges.

'How old is the baby?' said the judge.

'Eight weeks, *Herr Vorsitzender*,' said Sophie.

'What's the baby's name, Frau Auerbach?' said the judge.

At that moment, Maximilian hurried into the courtroom with the baby in his arms.

'Maria Christine,' said Sophie. Hearing her mother's voice, Maria Christine started to cry and worked her first miracle: Sophie was released on bail. 'But you may not leave Munich before the trial, Frau Auerbach, except with the court's permission. Is that clear?'

'Yes, *Herr Vorsitzender*.'

The trial was scheduled to take place in early October, before three judges: a presiding judge along with two lay judges, as was usually the case for serious crimes. The judges now had eight weeks to study the case, and Robert Fitzmorris had time to plan his strategy and line up witnesses.

Sophie passed the rest of the summer in Munich. The days were sunny and warm and she took Maria Christine on long walks under the linden trees along the broad boulevards and beside the Isar. People sat in the grass along the banks of the river. On hot days they rolled up their sleeves and lay back facing the sun with their eyes closed.

She ambled through the Nymphenburg Palace Park pushing Maria Christine, taking a path just because it pleased her to do so. People stopped to peer into the stroller, to ask the baby's name,

to ask how old she was. They then invariably told Sophie about
a baby in their life. Despite everything, Sophie was happy.

When the trial opened, Sophie sat with Robert Fitzmorris facing
the judges in their red robes. Maximilian was to be called as a
witness, so he could not be in the courtroom. The prosecution
presented their case, which was based almost entirely on the testimony of Jürgen Veit and Karl Meier. Both men had new haircuts
and wore ill-fitting suits. They had been carefully coached by the
prosecutor, which seemed to have the effect of making them even
more uneasy than they had been before. They fidgeted in their
seats and couldn't figure out what to do with their hands.

Questioned by the chief judge, both men swore that they had
been out for a stroll with Konrad Milch when they came upon
Maximilian and Sophie in the English Garden and that she had
shot Konrad as they passed by. 'What was your reaction?' said
the judge. Both men said they had run away. 'She was going to
shoot us too.'

'So, let me get this straight,' said Fitzmorris when he was
allowed to cross-examine Veit and then Meier, 'you're saying the
three of you were strolling in the middle of the night, minding
your own business, and this woman pulled out a pistol and shot
Konrad Milch without provocation?'

'That's right.'

'And why did you run away again?'

'I told you. I didn't want to get shot, man. She was crazy.'

'You were in a cafe before you went for your stroll, weren't
you?'

'Yes.'

'You saw the accused leave an art gallery and followed her into
the park, didn't you?'

'Like I said, we were . . .'

'You were arrested not too long ago, weren't you? In a pool
hall?'

'Yes.'

'What was your reaction when the police officer identified
himself as a police officer?'

Jürgen shifted this way and that on his chair. 'I was just minding
my own business.'

'You charged him with a knife, didn't you?'

'Well, he had a gun. I was defending myself. How did I know he was really a cop?'

The judge read aloud the long list of Jürgen Veit's arrests, following each citation with the question, 'And were you found guilty as charged?' To which Veit and then, when his turn came, Meier, had no choice but to answer, 'Yes, *Herr Vorsitzender.*'

'Did you know that Konrad Milch had a record of arrests?'

'No, *Herr Vorsitzender.*'

'You didn't know?'

'No, *Herr Vorsitzender.* He never told us . . . me.'

'So three convicted criminals are out for a stroll and are attacked by a small woman for no apparent reason?'

'That's the way it happened, judge.'

'*Herr Vorsitzender,*' the judge reminded him.

'That's the way it happened, *Herr Vorsitzender.*'

'Were any of you carrying weapons that evening?'

'No, *Herr Vorsitzender.* We were just out for . . .'

'Did you know Konrad Milch was carrying an unregistered pistol and a heavy metal pipe?'

'No, *Herr Vorsitzender*, I didn't know.'

The bailiff brought out the pipe and pistol and laid them on the exhibit table with a thump.

'That's a heavy pipe at least a half-meter long, and you didn't know he had it with him? Did he have it hidden in his pants or what?'

'I don't know, *Herr Vorsitzender.*'

'After Frau Auerbach shot and killed Konrad Milch, did you notify the police?'

'No, *Herr Vorsitzender.*'

'Once the crime was reported, did you come forth as witnesses?'

'No, *Herr Vorsitzender.*'

'And why didn't you come forward?'

'We would have, *Herr Vorsitzender*, but . . .'

'Was it your idea to have false witnesses come forward in your place?'

Veit and Meier were dismissed by the presiding judge with the notification that, given their testimony, they could both be expected to be charged with aggravated assault, obstruction of justice, and perjury. 'Get yourself a lawyer,' said the judge.

The judges called Maximilian to the stand. He told how they

had been attacked that night, and how Sophie had shot Milch and saved his life.

'Did you know Konrad Milch before he attacked you?' asked the presiding judge.

'I knew who he was, *Herr Vorsitzender*. He had attacked me once before.'

'When did he attack you the first time?'

'It was six years ago, November 9, 1923.'

'You remember the exact day?'

'It was the day after the Putsch. He was marching with Adolf Hitler.'

'Do you know why he attacked you? Did he give any reason?'

'No, *Herr Vorsitzender*, he didn't give me any reason, but I think it was because I was drawing his picture.'

The judges looked at one another in puzzlement. 'Herr Wolf is an artist for the *Munich Post, Herr Vorsitzender*,' said Robert Fitzmorris. 'He does drawings of life in and around Munich, and in that capacity was following the protests that day.'

The prosecutor wanted to know why Maximilian went around drawing pictures of strangers and whether that wasn't an aggressive act. Maximilian said it was not an aggressive act. The prosecutor asked whether Maximilian had ever killed a man. Maximilian said that he had in the war.

Sophie was called and sworn in and was led through her version of events by the presiding judge and Robert Fitzmorris. The prosecutor tried to discredit her story, but once again he didn't have anything to work with. He had tracked down Irena Milch and brought her to Munich for the trial. She was a sympathetic woman with a broad open face and gray hair. She testified to Konrad's having been abused by his father over and over again. Robert Fitzmorris asked Irena whether Konrad had ever attacked his father. Irena said that he had. She turned to the judge and, with tears welling in her eyes, said she was sorry for all the trouble her brother had caused.

None of the three judges approved of the *Munich Post*'s leftist politics, and learning that it was Maximilian who drew those distasteful pictures did not endear him to them. Nor did they like the idea of a woman walking around armed with a pistol, even one that was registered. And they were incredulous when she testified that she had thrown it in the Isar. Still, all the evidence seemed to demonstrate that she and Maximilian had been attacked and not the other way around. And given the flimsy case the prosecution had presented, they had no choice but to find Sophie not guilty of the charge.

'Frau Auerbach,' said the presiding judge, 'you are free to go.'

THE LYING PRESS

When the American stock market collapsed – it was just weeks after Sophie Auerbach's acquittal – vast swaths of wealth were wiped out in a matter of days. There were runs on American banks which then collapsed. The watching world was stunned by events into a sort of uncomprehending stupor, as though they were seeing a tsunami rising above the horizon that they knew, despite its static appearance, was certain to inundate and drown them all. It was the onset of the Great Depression. There was no high ground where anyone could be safe. Even economies that had seemed solid were crushed into splinters.

The German economy had not seemed solid. It had been propped up by American investments, which disappeared overnight. Not only that, but America started calling in loans. German industry – great and small – collapsed on a massive scale. In a very short time more than a third of the German workforce was out of work. Property was foreclosed upon, bankruptcies soared. And suicide became a common event.

Maximilian wandered the city drawing emaciated people in ragged clothes as they stood in line for food. He drew hands cradling shallow bowls of gruel, men scouring the gutter for cigarette butts, a man wearing a sandwich board that read *will work for food*, a young woman leading her small emaciated child by the hand as she solicited men. Another woman held a child to her breast, but the child looked dead. He drew people where they lived, in shantytowns thrown up beside railroad yards or in parks that had fallen into neglect. Maximilian drew as if his life depended on it, and in a sense it did. As it had been in the trenches, drawing was his salvation. As he drew a woman tying rags around her feet, he was doing the only thing he knew how to do. He was bearing witness to the suffering.

The government in Berlin was paralyzed. Fearing a return of inflation, which remained vivid in their memory, even more than their fear of massive unemployment, they did the worst thing they could have done: they reduced government spending and raised taxes, which only increased the suffering on the streets.

'I'm sorry, my boy,' said Aaron Appelbaum one afternoon. He and Maximilian sat in the gallery sipping tea. They had been looking through Maximilian's recent drawings. It was a raw, windy day. The trees were mostly bare, dead leaves circled in the street below them in frantic eddies. A man sat on the curb, his head in his hands. The sun was shining, but it gave no warmth. Aaron shook his head. 'These would make a wonderful show, Maximilian. But, I regret to say, I have to close the London gallery. New York too. At least for now. And in all honesty, I don't know whether they'll ever open again.'

Maximilian now derived an important part of his income from the Appelbaum Gallery. 'And Munich and Berlin?' he said.

'I'll keep Munich open. For now. Probably not Berlin. It's really no use. Nobody's buying art, my boy. Nor are they likely to any time soon. I'm really sorry. I truly love and admire your work. And when times change . . .' He took Maximilian's hand in both of his. 'Can I help you out in any way? Is the newspaper still . . .?'

'Yes,' said Maximilian. 'For the moment. They've kept us on. We're all right for the time being.'

Maximilian and Sophie were among the lucky ones. They still had jobs. The *Post* didn't lay anybody off. Everybody agreed to a thirty percent pay cut. 'We'll go for as long as we can,' said the publisher at an emergency staff meeting. 'We *have* to. Our work is too essential to stop. We're in the midst of an international catastrophe, and a national one as well. I don't think I have to tell you, this moment plays right into Adolf Hitler's hands.' He was right; this was the moment Hitler had been waiting for.

After being released from prison, Adolf Hitler had believed he could drive his supporters toward victory by his example, especially once President Held had restored the NSDAP to legitimacy. His reentry into the political arena was spectacular and defiant. He gave a speech at the Bürgerbräukeller, the same hall where he had engineered his Putsch two years earlier. The crowd was raucous, nearly hysterical. And Hitler did not disappoint. He cursed the government in Berlin and excoriated the Jews.

But, despite this debut, his Party was in serious trouble. Feuding factions were dividing and weakening the NSDAP. He admonished them for the sake of the Party and the Fatherland. But instead of resolving their squabbles, his seizing control of the Party had freed them to devote full energy to their power struggles.

Not only that, but as a result of that incendiary speech, his very first speech since coming out of prison, Hitler had been forbidden by the Bavarian government from speaking in public. Most of the rest of the German states had followed suit. He was allowed to speak in private gatherings, and he continued to do so, rallying the faithful in private halls and small gatherings, persuading roomfuls of wealthy donors to support his Party's resistance against Bolsheviks and Jews bent on destroying Germany and Western civilization. But having his voice missing from public forums could only hasten the Party's descent into oblivion.

The number of paying Party members continued to go down. In fact, by early 1927 the Party and Hitler were seen as a negligible factor in German society and politics. He was deemed so harmless that the Bavarian government restored his right to speak in public. Other state governments followed suit. What harm could he possibly do? He was saying the same old tired stuff in half-empty halls.

Only a few voices, the *Munich Post* among them, continued to sound the alarm. Sophie reported from a rally in Augsburg:

The Party faithful were there and they greeted their 'Führer' with happy cries of 'Heil! Heil!' Hitler did not fail to deliver the same lies and hateful rhetoric as he has for years now: the November criminals, the sick government in Berlin, and of course The Jew as evil incarnate. The Jew, he said, is to blame for everything that was wrong in Germany, when, in fact, it is Hitler who represents what is wrong with Germany, preying on ignorant and gullible minds, sowing discord, attacking the free press, and spreading venomous lies about our democracy.

We were approached by four thugs in brown shirts and told in no uncertain terms that if we did not leave immediately, they could not answer for our safety. At that moment Hitler pointed in our direction and said, 'See them? There they are like cockroaches. The Munich Post, *the so-called free press, a pack of liars.' We left amidst hoots from the crowd of 'Lügenpresse! Lügenpresse!'*

Everyone is saying he is finished. His day is past. But beware, readers: he is not finished and will not be finished so easily as that. He may be insane. But he is resourceful. And he is determined.

THE EVIDENCE ROOM

When Bergemann knocked on Willi's door this time, it was not entirely unexpected. In light of all the street unrest and the drastic budget cuts in the police department, a suspended police detective was a luxury the department could not afford. The order came down to put Willi Geismeier back to work. Bergemann, seen as the closest thing to a friend Willi had in the department, was chosen to deliver the news. 'You're reinstated, Willi,' he said as soon as Willi opened the door.

'Why?' said Willi. Not thanks, but 'why'.

'It's a desk job, though,' said Bergemann. He didn't know how to break it gently. 'In Central Records.'

'Central Records? Doing what?' said Willi.

'They'll tell you when you get there,' said Bergemann. 'You can always reapply for a detective spot. But . . . I wouldn't hold my breath. Everybody's being cut back. We're down to four detectives, and with the same caseload. Bigger really, since crime is up.'

Willi had been reduced in rank to *Wachtmeister* – constable, the lowest rank. He was ordered to go to Central Records at Police Headquarters the next morning. Sergeant Ludwig Marschach was in charge, if you could call it that, since he and Willi would be the only men in the department. Marschach was a former detective sergeant with thirty-five years on the force. He had been a decent detective at one time but had succumbed to alcohol. He had been disciplined multiple times for being drunk on duty and had finally been exiled to the basement at Ettstraße 2, where he could drink to his heart's content.

Willi descended the stairs to the basement. Sergeant Marschach was dozing at a battered steel desk behind a metal fence. As Willi closed the gate with a clang, the sergeant's red-rimmed eyes slowly opened. He took a deep breath through his nose, sucked on what remained of his teeth, and tried not quite successfully to sit up straighter. 'The new man?' he growled.

The basement had low ceilings with dim caged lights casting their gloom over rows of shelves from one end of the vast space to the other. The shelves were stacked floor to ceiling with cartons of files and who knew what else. 'You'll be back in Evidence,' said the sergeant, pointing vaguely down the narrow aisle into the darkness behind him. 'Back there. The desk with all the boxes on it.'

'And?' said Willi.

'File them,' said the sergeant.

Willi's job was to bring order to the Evidence Room, which was a section of the Records Department and not actually a separate room. Everything that was categorized as evidence – logs, testimony, exhibits – was supposed to be stored by case number, and was now his responsibility. As evidence moved in and out of the Evidence Room, things naturally got out of order and ended up stacked here and there waiting to be shelved in the proper place.

Willi sat down at the desk and, as the first thing, filled out the transfer request he had brought with him. He signed it, folded it, put it in an envelope, which he slid into his coat pocket. The desk and an adjoining table were loaded with items to be put away. There was more under the table and against the wall. It had been weeks since anything had been filed.

Whoever had dreamed up this assignment had meant to bury Willi, to exile him far from all police business. But it didn't take Willi very long to realize that he had been cast into a gold mine. Every single crime that had ever been committed in Munich was in some form or other documented here. And, to Willi's surprise, not only was the filing system simple and efficient, everything had been cross-referenced with related crimes and entered by a neat and legible hand into a master index. Willi's recently retired predecessor in this job had spent his entire career in Evidence. Evidence had been his calling and he had never wanted to be anywhere else. Order was his passion and he had made organizing the Evidence Room his life's work. If you knew what you were looking for, you could find it. In fact, you could pretty well find anything you needed to know about any crime.

A week or so after Willi had arrived and the backlog had been put in its place, he began researching Otto Bruck's extensive record. The pertinent files made a sizable stack, and he began to read. The list of Bruck's arrests had been known to Willi. But the notes by the investigating officers were new to him and very revealing. There were critiques of investigations written by senior police officials, which was not unheard of. But he also found records of official tampering, efforts to undermine an investigation so that things fell out in Otto Bruck's favor. Some officials, presumably assuming the files would never be revisited, had documented these unlawful efforts, noting conversations with this person or that or even with Bruck himself.

Everywhere he looked he found examples of official malfeasance, documented in many instances by the perpetrator himself. Konrad Milch's files, for instance, when he found them, contained letters and written testimony by SA and police officials alike meant to protect Milch from prosecution, all signed and dated. There was a letter from a judge declining to prosecute Milch because of his 'useful political engagement'.

Willi had at his disposal a massive record of government and police corruption and crime. Here was the legendary German propensity for order and thoroughness in full bloom. He held his arms out in front of him as though he were measuring the weight of this extraordinary new . . . what was it? A weapon? It felt as though he were holding a machine gun again.

'Leave it alone, Willi,' said Benno von Horvath. The two men sat in Benno's living room. Willi hadn't known who else he could talk to, who else he could trust.

'How can I leave it alone?' said Willi. 'This is criminal activity and I'm a policeman.'

'You have to leave it alone,' said Benno. 'You really have no choice.'

Benno had no sway in the department any longer. But he knew the culture, knew how it used to be, and understood how it was now. 'There was a time when you could have taken it to a judge, but not now. It's too late for that. What you've found is too big. And you're too small.'

'Well, what about Bruck?' said Willi. 'Instead of blowing the whistle on the whole stinking mess, what if I just go for Bruck?'

'You know the answer to that yourself, Willi. If you go after Bruck, everyone will see where it comes from, and worse, they'll know what it means for them: that they're next. If you expose a little corruption, you expose it all. Pulling any thread starts the whole thing unraveling. A lot of people will come after you. I'm not just talking about your career here, Willi. I'm talking about your life.'

OBSESSED

'What have you been up to back there, Geismeier?' said Sergeant Marschach. Willi had just come in to work. The two men shook hands.

'Filing, Sergeant,' said Willi. 'What else?'

'OK. If you say so.' Every policeman Marschach had ever known was trying to get away with something. Geismeier had obviously been sent to the Evidence Room as punishment for something, although Marschach didn't know what it was and didn't care, as long as Willi did the job and left Marschach alone. Whatever else he was, Geismeier certainly wasn't the record-keeping type. 'Just so you know, Geismeier: there was a captain back there last night, poking around.'

'What was he looking for?'

Marschach shrugged. 'He didn't say. He knew you, though. Mentioned you by name.'

'Who was it?' said Willi.

Marschach held up the sign-in sheet for Willi to read. Reineke.

'Thanks,' said Willi.

'No problem.' Marschach took a drink and lowered the bottle back into the drawer. 'Said he was a friend of yours.'

'Thanks,' said Willi again.

One morning on his way to work Willi got off the streetcar and came face to face with a poster. It had a red border with black swastikas in the corners, the slogan *DEUTSCHLAND FÜR DIE DEUTSCHEN* along the top in thick, black letters, and the stern face of Otto Bruck staring out at him. Bruck was running for a seat in the Reichstag as the NSDAP candidate, the Hitler candidate. The election was ten weeks away.

In the following days Willi saw more and more of Bruck's posters. They were everywhere. And there were young men on street corners wearing short pants, brown shirts, and red and black neckerchiefs, passing out his leaflets. 'A vote for Otto Bruck is a vote for Germany,' said a tall boy, maybe fifteen years old, with short, dark hair. He handed Willi a leaflet.

Bruck held rallies and drew large crowds. 'Many of us have given our flesh and blood for the Fatherland,' he said. 'And what do we have to show for it?' He held up his black hand. 'Nothing. What have we gotten from Berlin? Corruption and betrayal. And now, a great depression. If you're out of work, you're hungry, you're homeless, you have Berlin to thank.' The crowd mumbled and muttered. 'You're goddamn right,' someone shouted. 'Kill the bastards,' someone else shouted.

'Unemployment, hunger,' said Bruck, 'when we should be the greatest nation on earth. Where are the jobs they promised? When he's in power, Adolf Hitler will create millions of jobs. He'll bring prosperity back to Germany. If you send me to the Reichstag, together we'll help the Führer take over. We'll get rid of the crooked politicians. We'll make Germany great again.' After the rally had dispersed, a man in a ragged coat went around picking up the cigarette butts.

Every day Willi labeled new files and put away whatever had come in the previous day. He was usually finished filing before noon. He devoted the rest of the day to his research. Otto Bruck was his north star. Willi found Bruck's aliases by chasing paper trails. He found Bruck's confederates – criminal and police – in the same way and followed leads out from them as well. Willi was assembling the grandest scenario of all, an intricate map – no, a veritable atlas of the Munich police department's corruption and criminality.

Inevitably Willi came across an interesting cold case. A few years back, an office belonging to a minor right-wing party, a rival to the NSDAP, had been bombed. Someone had rolled a hand grenade through the office door and three political workers had been killed. A dozen others were injured. A suspect, a visiting 'businessman', who identified himself as Hans Dieter Gensler, had been spotted coming out of the building. Gensler was interrogated, and then promptly disappeared. Three men, though they could not say where he was now, swore they had been on a fishing trip with him the day of the bombing. A small hotel in the Black Forest confirmed their story. No one had been arrested for this bombing, and no charges had ever been filed. The name of one of the three alibi witnesses sounded familiar to Willi: Werner Schneidermann. Then it came to him: Werner Schneidermann was the student who had tormented Fedor Blaskowitz.

Detective Hans Bergemann was tired. Today had been rough. He needed to unwind. The walk home would do him good. Sergeant Gruber was all over him lately, ever since he had finally been invited to join the SS. Divorcing his wife Mitzi had done the trick. 'You have to divorce her, Gruber, if you want to get ahead,' Captain Reineke had told him. And he was right.

Today Gruber had been on his back about four people posing as a family and robbing people in the Munich Central Station and on the Marienplatz out front. They'd surround a mark – man or woman, ask for directions, and then pull a gun. 'It shouldn't be that hard, Bergemann. A man, a woman, a boy, and a girl robbing travelers in the middle of a crowd in broad daylight?'

'The crowd's the problem, Sergeant,' said Bergemann. 'They hide in the crowd. The whole thing's over in seconds. They go different directions and disappear in the crowd. Even if the mark shouts for help, the thieves are gone before anyone pays any attention. The noise is impossible, Sergeant. Did you ever try to meet anybody down there? It's hard to find people, even when you know what they look like.'

'Damn it, Bergemann, you've got descriptions. You're a detective, for Christ's sake.'

'Yeah, we've got descriptions, Sergeant. The man is tall with dark hair; no, he's bald. She's short and fat; no, she's skinny and pretty. He's sixty; no, he's forty. The kid is fourteen; no, he's twenty. The same with the girl. You know how witnesses are, Sergeant.'

'We've got six uniforms in the station, goddam it. Get back down there and arrest somebody.'

Bergemann turned into his street. The block was empty. He heard steps behind him. 'This is for you,' said a man, and pushed an envelope under his arm as he hurried past. Bergemann looked at the envelope. It had his name on it in large block letters. When he looked up, the man was gone. He looked at the envelope again. It was obviously from Geismeier. 'This is all I need,' he said with a groan.

* * *

The envelope contained a number of pages which were, according to the heading on the first page, a copy of the Gensler file including witness statements and a summary of Gensler's own statement. There was also a letter in which Willi had written that Hans Dieter Gensler and Otto Bruck were the same person, and that Werner Schneidermann had been one of Bruck's students.

'God, that man is obsessed,' said Bergemann.

'Did you say something, *Liebchen*?' said his wife from the kitchen. Smells of *Sauerbraten* were filling the room.

'No, dear,' said Bergemann. 'It's nothing.'

SEPTEMBER 14, 1930

A gong signaled the hour. *'It is eight p.m. This is Bavarian Radio. Good evening, ladies and gentlemen. Here is the news.*

'The votes have been counted in yesterday's Reichstag election, and in a political upset of epic proportions, the National Socialist German Workers' Party, the NSDAP, appear to have exceeded all expectations. They have received more than 6,371,000 votes. That is 18.5 percent of the total votes cast. This outcome catapults Adolf Hitler's NSDAP from being the smallest party in the Reichstag with twelve seats to being the second largest party with 107 seats. The Social Democrats remain the largest party with 143 seats, despite having lost ten seats. The KPD, the Communists, also gained seats, now having 54. Make no mistake, though, this is a resounding defeat for the SPD. And the big story is the shift to Adolf Hitler and the National Socialist German Workers' Party. This is a victory that must have taken even them by surprise. Once again, they have received more than 6,371,000 votes and have won 107 seats in the Reichstag.'

The news report was followed by a discussion among a panel of journalists and political scientists about the causes and effects of this political earthquake. They debated what effect last year's Wall Street crash might have had, how it had brought American investment in Germany to an end.

Had the collapse of the German economy been inevitable or could it have been prevented? What could have been done to stem the massive unemployment that had ensued? Anger at the Social Democratic mismanagement of things in Berlin had pushed voters toward the political extremes. The rise of these extremes and the demise of the political center had led to renewed unrest, food shortages, people fighting in the streets. It was like 1919 all over again.

'The economy explains it,' said the moderator, 'but only in part. This is a massive change in the political landscape, isn't it? Was it coming in any case? Just how did the NSDAP manage to pull it off? Was it fear-mongering that did it?'

'No, no,' said one panelist. 'Not at all. We have to face it: Adolf

Hitler is a political genius. He took the correct measure of German society, then organized a brilliant campaign. He and his Party spoke to all the issues that concern ordinary German citizens today: jobs, security, a stable economy. And he spoke to them in a language they could understand. The Social Democrats and the Centrists missed the boat completely.'

'Well, he's a genius, if you call lying and intimidation genius. I mean, he made up "facts" that had no bearing on reality, his supporters beat up and intimidated their opponents . . .'

'Oh, come on. Whatever you think of his politics, this campaign was perfectly organized. He turned out his voters all across Germany, people who have been left behind, who are unemployed, and they don't see jobs coming back.'

'Well, that may all be true,' said someone else. 'But when it comes down to it, what can Adolf Hitler or anyone else do about that?'

'There's plenty he, or anyone else, can do. Our industry is in ruins. Our infrastructure is crumbling from neglect. Look at the state of our roads and bridges. The armed forces have been downsized into insignificance. Our weapons systems are obsolete, insufficient to defend ourselves. Turning around any one of these things will create massive numbers of new jobs, and that will turn the economy around.'

'Maybe you forget: the army is already larger than it is allowed to be according to the treaty we signed. We are forbidden, again by treaty, from rearming—'

'Signing Versailles was a criminal act. That treaty had one purpose, and one purpose only, and that was to crush Germany. That's what it was meant to do, and in that it has succeeded. That any German signed Versailles . . . it was an outrageous act of treachery. Treason, that's what it was.'

Otto Bruck was elected to the Reichstag from Munich's Northern District by a substantial margin. He and his supporters celebrated at Party headquarters. People were cheering, pumping their fists, drinking, laughing, and slapping one another on the back. Bruck had won even though a series of articles in the *Munich Post* had accused him of several crimes, 'not unsolved so much as unprosecuted, thanks largely to corruption in the police department and the judiciary'.

Otto Bruck thanked his supporters for all their hard work, for turning out voters. 'That was the key, you know, my friends. You came out, and you voted. Despite the lies and slanders of the Jewish *Pest* and their fake news . . .'

'Don't let them get away with it!' somebody shouted. 'Lock them up!' shouted someone else, and others chimed in. 'Lock them up. Lock them up.'

Otto lifted his hands to calm down the crowd. 'Don't worry, my friends. They won't get away with it. We're taking power from the Jews, in Berlin, in the press and everywhere else, and we're returning it to you, the German people. The *authentic* German people. Thanks to the Führer, we will soon rule Germany. *Deutschland für die Deutschen! Heil Hitler!*' They raised their arms in the Hitler salute and cheered.

The following week Adolf Hitler held a meeting with the new Reichstag members from Bavaria. He knew the Munich members, Otto Bruck among them, personally. He offered them his congratulations, thanked them for their devotion to the Fatherland, and promised them that the day was near when true Germans would again rule Germany. The Communists and the Jews, all the enemies of Germany would be dealt with.

'And the press, *Mein Führer*?' said Otto Bruck. He was still smarting from the articles in the *Munich Post*.

For the last dozen years Hitler too had been locked in a state of war with the press, and most particularly with the *Munich Post*. His attorneys had been filing and mostly losing lawsuits against the paper. Hitler had even sent his storm troopers to attack their offices, all to no avail. The *Post* had relentlessly attacked Hitler and the NSDAP as a criminal enterprise, reporting on their physical violence, intimidation, and eventually on their intention to get rid of the Jews. The *Post* had gone after all of Munich's Reichstag candidates, but none so forcefully as Otto Bruck.

'It has not gone unnoticed that you were crucified by the Jew press,' said Hitler, looking at Bruck. 'I promise you that this poison kitchen' – *die Giftküche* was his name for the *Post* – 'won't survive our ascent to power. They will be wiped from the face of the earth.' Which was what eventually happened.

SERGEANT LUDWIG MARSCHACH

Sergeant Ludwig Marschach was often asleep when Willi arrived at work in the morning. And he was often asleep when he left in the evening. Maybe, Willi thought, he's always here; maybe he lives here. One morning Willi started to tiptoe past as he often did. 'Geismeier,' said the sergeant. 'A word.' He had the *Munich Post* in front of him open to the article about Otto Bruck.

'Yes, Sergeant?' said Willi.

Marschach rubbed his eyes. 'Is this you, Geismeier?' he said, tapping the paper with the back of his hand.

Willi leaned in and looked at the article. 'Sergeant?' he said.

'Is . . . this . . . you,' said the sergeant as though he were talking to a six-year-old.

'What do you mean, Sergeant?'

Marschach scratched his head with both hands, rubbed his eyes again, cracked his knuckles one by one. He really had just woken up.

'I mean,' he said, 'is the information in this article about Otto Bruck based on research you've been doing here in the Evidence Room when you were supposed to be working?'

'No, Sergeant, it isn't.'

Sergeant Marschach gazed at Willi with his small red eyes. He rubbed his grizzled chin thoughtfully. 'OK, Geismeier. If you say so.' He opened the drawer where his bottle was stored. 'Drink?' he said.

'No, thank you, Sergeant.'

'OK, Geismeier. Carry on.'

Willi went straight to his research notes, which by now were a thick packet of papers. He kept them in a particularly dusty and inaccessible corner of the Evidence Room no one was ever likely to visit. Each evening before he left, he tucked them away in such a way that he would immediately see the following morning whether they were as he had left them. This morning they were not as he had left them. Someone had taken them out, been through them, and then put them back in a particularly haphazard fashion, almost as though they wanted him to know he had been found out.

'Sergeant?' said Willi. 'A word.'

'Christ, Geismeier, you scared me. Don't sneak up on me like that. What is it?'

'I'm wondering why you asked me about the article in the *Post*.' Willi held the bundle of research notes under his arm.

Sergeant Marschach nodded toward the bundle. 'That's why,' he said.

'I'm surprised you found them. I should have been more careful.'

'I was once a pretty good detective, Geismeier. I heard all about you after you got here. I heard you were a good detective. And I heard you'd been going after Bruck.'

'You know Bruck?'

'Not personally, no.'

'But you know about him,' said Willi.

'Oh, yeah, I know about him.'

'And what do you know?'

'Well,' said the sergeant, nodding again toward the bundle of papers, 'a good bit more than I did yesterday. You've done a lot of excellent research. To think this stuff was all here this whole time. I'm really impressed.'

Willi took a stab in the dark. 'But you know something I don't know.'

Sergeant Marschach went silent. After a while he said, 'Keep up the good work, Geismeier. You've given me plenty to think about.'

The next morning Willi found a yellowed newspaper clipping on his desk dated April 19, 1919, describing how a police detective had arrived home one morning after working the night shift to find his wife and infant daughter murdered in their beds. The woman, Ingeborg Marschach, had been raped before being stabbed multiple times with a kitchen knife. There was one suspect, but he had an alibi, and the case went cold.

Willi found the case file. The suspect, unnamed in the newspaper clipping, was Hans Dieter Gensler.

THE TEA KETTLE

Hans Bergemann thought long and hard about what to do with the file Willi had had his messenger tuck under his arm. He knew that anything he might try to do with the Bruck information would mean the end of his career, and surely Willi Geismeier had known that when he sent it. Bergemann also knew the file was almost certainly on its way to the *Post*, if it wasn't there already. So why had Willi sent it to him at all? Was it an admonition? Was it a trap? Was it a test of some sort? He opened the wood stove and fed the pages in one by one. He made sure the flames took them all and turned them to ash before he closed the door.

Bergemann watched the *Post* and, when the article came out, he brought the paper to Gruber. 'I thought you should see this, Sergeant.' A short time later Sergeant Gruber made several phone calls and then left the office with the paper under his arm. Bergemann then left the office himself. He walked a dozen blocks to a telephone booth. He dropped a coin in and dialed a number. A woman answered. She sounded like the woman he had seen at Willi's apartment. He asked to speak to Willi Geismeier.

'There's no one here by that name,' she said. But she didn't hang up.

'Tell him, please, that I called.' Bergemann hoped she would remember him. Still she didn't hang up.

'I'm sorry,' she said again, 'but there's no one here by that name.'

'Tell him that Gruber has taken the *Post* article to Reineke, and maybe further up the line. They know Willi's behind it. Tell him Gruber is connected to Tannenwald, the chief. And so is Bruck.' Bergemann had discovered this connection after Willi had been transferred to the Evidence Room, and he didn't know whether Willi knew it or not.

'You must have the wrong number,' she said. She still did not hang up.

'Tell him they're going to arrest him.'

There was silence at the other end of the line.

'OK. Good luck,' said Bergemann, and hung up the phone.

Gruber, looking out for himself as he always did, insisted the arrest be properly done. Geismeier had to be charged with a crime by the Bavarian State Prosecutor, then a warrant had to be issued by an investigating judge. Willi Geismeier was to be arrested at his home, Apartment 3-B, Penzigauerstraße 26.

Shortly after four o'clock on the morning of September 20 a squad of six men, two SS officers and four Munich city constables who were also in the SA, arrived at the building. It was a crystal-clear night, there was no moon, there was no wind, the air was frosty. The six men crept up the three flights of stairs.

Once they were in front of 3-B, the SS lieutenant in charge knocked hard on the door. They waited. There was no response. He knocked again, even harder and longer. They waited. The lieutenant nodded to one of the constables, who kicked the door once, then again. It flew open. The men rushed inside, reached for the light switch, then stopped in their tracks.

Not only was no one there, there was *nothing* there. There was no furniture, there were no carpets on the floor, no pictures on the wall, not even curtains or window shades. The other two rooms were just as empty, except for the small kitchen, which held what looked to be a brand-new gas stove, all shiny white enamel and steel. On one of the eyes of the stove sat a cast-iron tea kettle. After studying it from every side to make sure it wasn't booby trapped, the SS lieutenant in charge gingerly removed the lid. The other men took a step backwards. The lieutenant laid the lid aside, and picked up the kettle itself, turning it around, turning it upside down while the other men stood and watched.

'What the hell *is* this?' said the SS lieutenant.

'A tea kettle, sir,' said one of constables.

THE MUNICH POST

Aaron Appelbaum had closed all his galleries, finally even Munich, but had continued to buy and sell art out of his apartment. He had found a few buyers for Maximilian's drawings and paintings. And for a year now he had been shipping art to the United States. He had also been transferring money to a Swiss bank account. It was not a large amount, but it would be enough to get him started on a new life. His wife was dead, his only son was in Palestine. 'Come to Tel Aviv, Papa. It is the new frontier,' he wrote.

'I'm too old for the new frontier, Moishe,' Aaron responded. He left for the United States on January 30, 1933, the day Hitler was named Chancellor.

Maximilian went with him to the train to see him off. The station was busier than usual and there were SS men everywhere. Aaron walked with a cane now. A large steamer trunk had been shipped ahead. Maximilian carried his small suitcase. The train for Cologne and Rotterdam was announced. Aaron and Maximilian embraced. 'My dear boy,' said Aaron. 'If the moment comes when you want to or have to leave, bring your little family to New York. It is a great city. You'll be safe there, and you can have a normal life.' A normal life. What would that even be?

On March 9, 1933, unmarked trucks roared up to the offices of the *Munich Post* and stopped with a great screeching of brakes. One truck with a machine gun in back positioned itself at the entrance to the building. Armed SS men spilled out of the trucks and ran inside. They hurried past the receptionist and the secretaries, fanning out through the building. Within minutes they had arrested the editors and many of the editorial staff. They marched them out of the building with their hands held above their heads. They searched the business offices, gathering all the files in one place. Before the end of the day the files were removed and burned. All non-editorial employees – secretaries, couriers, maintenance people, typesetters, pressmen – had their personal information recorded. Then they were allowed to leave.

The empty building was padlocked and guarded by the SS. In

the following days trucks arrived. Crews removed the presses and other equipment to a great smelting foundry on the edge of the city where it was all destroyed. Adolf Hitler wanted the destruction of the *Munich Post* to be so complete that no one would ever think of it again. He even ordered the house number removed from the building and from the map and forbade its ever being used again.

The editorial staff were charged with sedition, treason, and anything else Hitler could think of. They were quickly tried and convicted. Some were summarily executed. Others were sent to prisons and concentration camps, like Dachau, which had recently opened.

Sophie was about to take Maria Christine to her kindergarten when she received a telephone call. A man's voice, one she didn't recognize, told her that an SS raid on the *Post*'s offices was about to begin.

'Who is this?' she said, but the man hung up. She tried to call the *Post*. All the numbers were busy. She was already late getting Maria Christine to her kindergarten, which was only a few blocks from the paper. After dropping the child off and walking a block, Sophie sensed something was wrong. There were SS men stationed on street corners. She went back to the kindergarten, got Maria Christine, and took her home. She called the paper again. This time the phone rang, but nobody picked up.

Willi Geismeier had given her a phone number to call in case of an emergency. She called it. 'Evidence and records,' said a man's voice. She thought it sounded like the voice that had called her at home to warn her. But then she thought she must be imagining things. Willi had told her to use only first names. 'I'd like to speak to Willi,' she said, 'this is Sophie.'

'Sophie,' said the man. 'Where are you?'

She hesitated.

'If you're at home, get out of there,' he said. 'The *Post* has been raided by the SS. Maximilian is waiting for you at his parents' house.'

'Who are you?' she said.

'I'm nobody,' he said, and she could have sworn he was weeping.

FOR INGEBORG

'You have a call, *Herr Hauptmann*.' Otto Bruck was a member of the Reichstag now and could use the title *Herr Abgeordneter*, Mr Deputy. But he had recently joined the SS as a captain, and captain was the title he preferred. He favored the black uniform now too. His peaked cap sat perched on the corner of the desk, where he could see the silver eagle holding the swastika and below it the death's head.

Otto had spent most of the last week in Munich, making the rounds to various high officials, wrapping up local business before moving to Berlin. He had a new staff in woeful need of training and discipline. There were lots of ribbon cuttings and other official celebrations to be attended to. Then when you added in all government and Party business, well, it was clear why interruptions were unwelcome.

'I told you no calls,' he said.

'I'm sorry, *Herr Hauptmann*, but this is one I think you'll want to take.'

'Who is it?' He glared at the young assistant, tapping his pen on the desk impatiently. 'What's so important?'

'It's the desk sergeant at the Police Records Department, sir. He says he has something very important.'

'The desk sergeant? Really? My God, isn't this something *you* know how to deal with?'

'No, sir. I don't think so. The sergeant said it was a matter having to do with your police record. I don't know what he . . .'

Otto picked up the phone. 'Yes? Who is this?' He waved the assistant out of the office.

'This is Sergeant Marschach, *Herr Hauptmann*. Central Records. I have something here, sir, that belongs to you.'

'Go on.'

'A policeman named Geismeier.'

Hearing the name caused Otto to sit up straighter.

'Constable Geismeier has, as you must know, been busy with

your, shall we say, history. He was working here in Records in
the Evidence Room until he disappeared . . .'

'He was arrested, wasn't he?'

'Well, he was supposed to be, sir, but he seems to have flown
the coop. Anyway, he was posted here in Records in the Evidence
Room for the last, oh, I don't know how long . . .'

'Get to the point, Sergeant!'

'Yes, sir. Geismeier was a lousy traitor, *Herr Hauptmann*, up
to no good. He was placed in charge of evidence, and he used
his time and the police files at his disposal – and I had no idea
what he was up to – to put together a record, *quite* a record of
your past . . . activities. I don't want to say any more over the
phone, *Herr Hauptmann*, but I think you probably know what
I'm talking about. So far, the information is contained here in the
Records Department.' Otto drummed his fingers impatiently on
the desk. 'I wanted to alert you, *Herr Hauptmann*, to Geismeier's
treachery. There's a stack of material here I'm sure you wouldn't
want to get into the wrong hands . . .'

'God damn it, Sergeant, what the hell are you saying? Are you
trying to blackmail me?'

'What? No. No, sir!' said Marschach. 'No. Good God, no. I
know you're in the Führer's circle, sir. This is information that
could harm you, sir, and the Führer. *You* should have this information. There are plenty of people that would like to do the new
government harm.'

Otto was suddenly aware that this was not the kind of conversation he wanted to have over the telephone. He didn't quite believe
the records sergeant was quite the harmless character he was
pretending to be. 'You did the right thing by calling, Sergeant. I
will come right over to Records. It's downstairs in Ettstraße, is
that right? Is anyone else there in Records with you?'

'No, sir, *Herr Hauptmann*. Not since Geismeier left. I'm running
the whole show. I could use some help, sir. It's too much for one
man. If . . .'

'Yes, yes, Sergeant. I understand. But as far as this matter goes,
it's just between us. No one else there. You give me what you've
got. I'll decide how to deal with it.'

'Deal with it? Of course, sir. I'm here until seven this evening.'

'No one else there, Sergeant. Understood?'

'Yes, sir, *Herr Hauptmann*.'

At 6:30 Otto pushed the buzzer to call an assistant. He ordered a car and a contingent of four SS men. He put on his overcoat. He took his holster from the coat rack and strapped it on. He wore his pistol on the left because of his hand.

Otto didn't think the sergeant was up to any tricks, but you couldn't be too careful. And depending on how much of a look he had had into Geismeier's files, well, he would have to be dealt with somehow too.

And Geismeier was a cunning character. What if he was there? Otto had to be prepared for anything. The police guards ushered Otto and his SS men into the headquarters building and pointed the way to the Records Department.

'You wait here,' said Otto to his SS contingent, as they reached the stairs. The fewer people that saw or heard what went on, the better.

Sergeant Ludwig Marschach was asleep at his desk. He was snoring. Otto Bruck rattled the fence that surrounded the Records Department and came through the gate. 'Sergeant!' he shouted. 'This is outrageous.'

Marschach snorted and blinked his eyes. He peered at Otto through tiny red eyes, as though he were trying to recognize him.

'SS Captain Otto Bruck, Sergeant!' said Bruck angrily.

'What? Oh, yes sir, *Herr Hauptmann*,' said Marschach. He struggled to sit up straight but made no effort to stand.

'I don't have a lot of time, Sergeant,' said Bruck. 'What is it you have for me?'

'Well, as I said on the phone, Herr Bruck . . .'

'Captain, Goddamnit!' said Bruck. 'Really, Sergeant. I'll see that you're written up for this.'

'Yes, sir, Herr Bruck.'

Bruck leaned toward the sergeant. 'Have you been drinking, Sergeant?'

'Yes, sir, I have.'

Bruck straightened to his full height. 'Are you *drunk*, Sergeant?'

'Yes, sir, I am.'

'What is the meaning of this, Sergeant?'

'The meaning, sir? It has no meaning.'

'Drinking on the job, is . . .'

'It's how I get through the day, *Herr* Captain. We all have our own way of getting through the day, don't we?'

'Let's get this over with, shall we? Where are the files, the Geismeier files . . .'

'How do you get through the day, *Herr* Captain Otto Bruck?'

'I'll take those records, Sergeant. Right now.'

'Wouldn't you like a drink, sir?'

Marschach could see Bruck was losing all patience. 'All right, all right, *Herr* Captain.' He opened the middle drawer of the desk, pulled out a large pistol, and shot Otto Bruck right between the eyes. The sound reverberated through the building. The following silence was profound. Then came the sound of boots clattering down the stairs. The SS men and the police guards arrived to find Otto Bruck lying on his back jammed against the fence, his dead eyes wide open, his mouth too. A dark pool of blood was spreading rapidly across the concrete floor, so that the SS men had to jump out of the way to avoid getting it on their boots.

Sergeant Marschach stood up and handed the pistol to one of the guards. 'So, Ingeborg, my love,' he said softly. 'That's finally taken care of.'

THE THOUSAND-YEAR REICH

The Great War had been over for fifteen years. But it was still vivid in their recollection; they saw it around them and felt it in their bodies. The very ground they stood on sometimes seemed to go liquid and give way under their feet. Margarete von Horvath felt it more than Benno. Margarete would be standing or walking and would suddenly feel unsteady and reach out for something or someone – Benno – to hold on to.

Their lives had shrunken. Their charming social evenings with champagne and cold buffets and lively discussion belonged to another world. They saw no one; they kept to themselves. Their friends had scattered. Willi Geismeier seemed to have disappeared.

Something new and monstrous lay just ahead. You could smell it, taste it – acrid, like gunpowder. Its signs were everywhere. They knew, at least Benno did, it would soon be overhead, would come crashing down and crush them to smithereens. You could feel it approaching. You just couldn't quite name it yet. It hadn't yet taken on specific shape. So you could still hurry on your way, looking neither right nor left and pretend things were otherwise.

It arrived as men marching. First you heard them, then you saw their brown uniforms, their faces like masks. Their torches rose and fell in unison, black smoke rising, a hypnotic harbinger of the destruction they would inflict and that would then consume them too. Once you *could* see such things, you chose not to. How else to survive?

'Come away from the window, Margarete,' said Benno. The reflected torchlight flickered and danced on the ceiling, and he drew the curtains closed.

'What does it mean, Benno?'

'Well, he has become Chancellor,' said Benno. 'We shall see soon enough what it means.' He was thinking, though, *It is the beginning of the end of Germany. Now he can do whatever he wants. He can attack or kill or persecute. Whatever he wants. This will be the hardest thing we ever face.*

Benno von Horvath had fallen in love with Margarete Bertelmann the moment he first saw her, before she had even spoken a word to him. That had been at a party celebrating the new century when they were students at the University of Vienna, a moment thirty-three years ago that already seemed lost in history. And, to his own astonishment, he had never moved beyond that first moment of love; he was as enchanted by her presence now as he had been that first day.

Benno still thought of Margarete's wellbeing and happiness as his first and principal duty. In the many years of their marriage he had never once wavered from this obligation. It was Benno's extraordinary good luck that the fulfillment of this duty provided him with the greatest joy he had ever known. *How many people are so fortunate as to enjoy more than anything that which they are obliged to do?* he thought.

Benno was not a romantic; he was of this world. He was well acquainted with the ugliest aspects of human existence. He had been a policeman. He had seen up close the worst things human beings can do to one another. He had lived through the Great War and its violent aftermath. He had lived through the Great Depression when people were starving in the streets and the Nazis were on the rise. By now he had no illusions about whether Hitler would seize power and what he would do once he had it.

Surprisingly, though, as bleak as the world seemed to him, Benno did not have a dark or pessimistic approach to life. In fact, his life with Margarete allowed him, no, *required* him, to live life as an optimist. Because of her, he had worked as best he could for the betterment of man. He had been a conscientious policeman and a dutiful and generous citizen. And now he found himself obliged to resist however he could the evil that was taking over. Contrary to what one might imagine, this obligation lifted him out of darkness. This was Margarete's gift to him, and, Benno realized, it was the greatest gift anyone could receive.

Margarete believed in the essential kindness of human beings because she was herself incapable of anything but kindness and incapable of imagining anything else in others. This was a wondrous blessing and a grievous fault. Of course, she saw in Hitler someone deranged and disturbed. But when he and the National Socialists began public works projects like the construction of the Autobahn highway system or the Winter Relief to feed, clothe, and house the poor, she had to see it as a good thing and a hopeful moment. How could you see it otherwise? Even the massive build-up of the army and the construction of great factories turning out planes, tanks, guns, bombs put millions of people back to work, put money in their pockets and food on the table. Hunger and depravity disappeared from the streets. How was that not a good thing?

Margarete worried deeply about the Jews and their persecution. She had Jewish cousins in Poland and in Austria. But she wondered whether, having brought Germany back from the depths of depression, Hitler might not now relent, might no longer need the Jewish scapegoat, might even find within himself a strain of kindness and mercy. 'After all,' she said, 'what is to be gained by belligerence and anger?'

It was not just Margarete who entertained such delusions. The whole German nation was wishing that what they saw coming was something else entirely. Even people less hobbled by kind spirits than Margarete was, even skeptics, cynics, religionists of all sorts embraced what was happening without seeing where it led.

People cheered the Führer whenever and wherever he appeared. They attended his massive rallies and raised their arms and shouted '*Heil, Hitler!*' in celebration. Red, white, and black flags flapped happily from masts and public buildings. More than ninety percent of Austrians voted to join the German Reich, which was, after all, where they belonged – with their own kind. Joyous masses filled the streets of Vienna when the German army rolled in. The Sudeten Germans in Czechoslovakia needed protection too, at least Hitler said so, and everyone was happy when the German army marched in. The rest of the world watched it happen and seemed satisfied. How could you argue with that?

From such beginnings, the war came on inevitably, relentlessly, almost like a natural thing, a gigantic living being, a great, violent, seething, roiling cloud, lethal and poisonous, evil and ruinous. It rolled over them and consumed them. It grew larger and larger and endured longer and longer, nourished, it seemed, by anything and everything it consumed. It ate people by the thousands.

The war weighed heavy on Margarete. 'Why Poland?' she said once it began for real. She was terrified. Her cousin Elsa in Krakow had not been heard from. A cold hand reached into her chest and squeezed her heart until she couldn't breathe. 'Why Poland?' she said again.

Benno held her hand. 'Because,' he said, but then was unable to find an answer that would satisfy both Margarete's hope and the truth. 'I hope Elsa is all right,' he said instead. 'She should be fine in Krakow.'

Their life was diminished more and more by the war until there was nothing left to it but the war itself. It was a great carapace they carried on their back. They were like snails being killed by their own shells. Everyone was. It didn't have to be, but the horrible truths that now hung in the air – that was how Benno saw the flags now, each one a stand-in for a lie, a brutality, an atrocity – kept you inside yourself. Friendships dissolved over the need to be alone, to hide until, who knows what. They listened to the BBC – their heads close to the radio so that the neighbors couldn't hear – where they heard about the extermination of Jews, shot in vast numbers and buried in mass graves, then in the new concentration camps. 'Auschwitz, Poland?' That was a place they had never heard of before.

'That can't be true, can it?' said Margarete. 'That's got to be propaganda, doesn't it? Oh, Benno, please . . .' She wept.

The German news spoke of great victories. Operation Barbarossa – the invasion of Russia – was a stellar success. The BBC spoke of Stalingrad, of tens of thousands of dead German soldiers, the rupturing of supply lines, the deadly winter where entire battalions of German soldiers froze to death, the mass surrenders of others, the gross incompetence and failures of Adolf Hitler and his generals, and the inevitable defeat of the German armies in the East.

In the greatest invasion ever, the Allies landed in Normandy. Six weeks later there was a loud knock on the door. Benno was arrested and taken away. There had been an attempt by German officers to assassinate Hitler. More than seven thousand suspects were arrested all over Germany. Many, like Benno, were never seen or heard from again.

Then the bombers came, waves of them, night after night. *Avenging angels*, Margarete thought. 'Take me,' she prayed. 'I was ignorant. That was a mortal sin. Take me.'

1945

The Americans had been in Munich a few weeks when First Lieutenant Tom O'Connor, US Army Intelligence, arrived. He had to maneuver his jeep through cratered, debris-littered streets. By the end of the war half the city had been damaged or destroyed in bombing raids. You would be going down a street, turn a corner and find total devastation, buildings reduced to piles of stone and shattered timbers. Or one wall would be standing inexplicably with its empty windows staring blindly into the ruin. Some streets were completely buried, so the lieutenant had to back up and find another way. Everywhere there were Germans picking through the rubble. Had they lived there, or were they just searching for something they could use or trade or sell?

Lieutenant O'Connor was part of the 74th Military Police Battalion, whose job it was to reestablish a German police force throughout the Zone of American Occupation and bring order back to German society. The 74th had its headquarters in Frankfurt with the Seventh Army, but they had attached O'Connor to a Military Police battalion in Munich.

'Basically, Munich was Nazi central,' said Major Becker, the MPs' operations officer. 'The police here were the worst of the worst. We don't know whether there were any decent cops at all by the end. So basically, O'Connor, we're starting from scratch. You and your guys have to find a new police force. We're looking for good cops from among a bunch of former Nazis. How many men do you have?'

'Six or eight,' said O'Connor. 'I'm not sure, sir. We'll see when they arrive.'

'Eight? Jesus. I hope they're good men,' said the major.

'I hope so too, Major. We'll just have to see.'

'OK, O'Connor. Any idea how you'll proceed?'

'No, sir, not really. I'll know better in a day or two.'

'OK, Lieutenant. For now we've got some Nazi cops on duty along with our men, but we've already had some problems. We need to build a new German police force top to bottom as fast as we can. We'll train them up, but it's up to you to find them.'

Lieutenant O'Connor was to set up operations in what had been the old Ettstraße police headquarters. He picked his way past piles of rubble into the building. He found a table and a couple of chairs in a corner and dragged them into the center of the entry hall. That was his office. Next to the entry hall he found a row of offices that would make adequate billets for his little detachment. Behind him were steps down to the old Records Department. He went down to have a look around. The shelves had been knocked over at some point and everything had been set ablaze, probably in an effort to destroy old records, although it might have been an incendiary bomb. He couldn't tell. The rest of the building was pretty much a bombed-out ruin.

Sergeant Owens showed up the next morning in a truck. He had scrounged a couple of army-issue steel desks, some tables, chairs, bunks, and a couple of typewriters. Owens had spent the last two years of the war interviewing prisoners of war and anyone else who was thought to have useful intelligence. He was supposed to be pretty good at it.

'Did you see action, Owens?' said O'Connor.

'Some, Lieutenant. You?'

'Some. You have some German, is that right?'

'Yes, sir. Not perfect, but good enough to work with.' Owens was a muscular kid with a handlebar mustache and an accent that sounded like Kentucky.

'Good. So, I understand we've already had some German cops showing up, wanting their jobs back. We're going to be interviewing these guys. I'm not sure what we're looking for exactly, but we'll figure it out as we go along.'

'OK, Lieutenant.'

'Some of them are liable to be Nazis. Maybe most of them.'

'So, you think they're coming in early because they're clean, or because they think we don't care if they were Nazis, or what?'

'Probably some of both. From what I hear about Munich, we're going to have to take on some old Nazis. Anyway, we'll just have to see.' Owens and O'Connor were walking from room to room, seeing what was habitable and what wasn't. O'Connor opened a door. It was a toilet. The plaster ceiling had pretty much fallen in. He pulled the chain and the toilet flushed. The two men listened silently as the tank filled up with water. 'Well, whadya know?' said O'Connor.

'Things are looking up,' said Owens.

Two days later six men showed up. Three had some interrogation experience, two were infantry men, and one was a medic. Lieutenant O'Connor explained their mission.

'How we gonna do that with six men, Lieutenant,' said Private Veroni, one of the infantry men.

'Eight,' said O'Connor. 'Sergeant Owens and I make eight.'

'OK, eight,' said Veroni. 'We gotta build a whole fucking police force? From nothin'? That's bullshit! It ain't gonna happen.'

'Oh, it's gonna happen, Veroni,' said Sergeant Owen. 'You know why? What's your MOS, Veroni?'

'Machine gunner, sir.'

'So, if it doesn't happen, it'll mean you didn't pull your weight. And you're gonna find your sorry ass carrying that big fucking machine gun up and down mountains out in the middle of fucking nowhere.'

Lieutenant O'Connor had one of the German policemen still on duty type an announcement that the police were hiring. Becker's clerk ran off a hundred copies on his mimeograph, and the MPs stuck them up around the city. Men showed up the next day wanting to apply. Some were even wearing their old police uniforms. They were given application forms to fill out. Hermann Gruber was among them.

Lieutenant O'Connor and Manfred Schultz, a German police captain, sat collecting the applications and doing interviews. Interviews went on all morning. Decisions were made in the afternoon, and hires were posted on a bulletin board, along with where they were to report for duty.

Manfred Schultz remembered seeing Gruber now and then at Nazi Party functions, although they hadn't known each other. 'Hermann Gruber's a good man,' he said.

'You speak English?' said Lieutenant O'Connor. Gruber had checked that box.

'Yes, sir!' said Gruber, but in fact he only had a few words, so they switched to German.

'You were a policeman until the end, weren't you, Herr Gruber?'

'Yes, sir.'

'And what was your job?'

'I was a detective sergeant in the Tenth District, sir.'

'How long were you in the force?'

'Over twenty years.'

'Do you have a family?'

'No, sir. No children. And I lost my wife, sir. She was Jewish. She was sent to Auschwitz in forty-four.'

O'Connor looked at Schultz. Schultz gave a slight nod to indicate it was true.

'So you weren't a Nazi, Gruber.'

'I joined the Party, sir. You had to, back then. But I wasn't a believer.'

'Were you in the SA?'

'No, sir.'

'Were you in the SS?'

'No, sir.'

'But a lot of your colleagues were.'

'Yes, sir,' said Gruber. 'And I know which ones, sir.'

O'Connor thought for a moment. 'OK, Gruber. I'd like you to help in our selection process. That involves sitting with us afternoons, going through applications, and making hires. You'd get a half-day's pay.'

'Do you trust him?' said Sergeant Owen that afternoon when the Lieutenant explained why Gruber was in the meeting.

'No,' said O'Connor. 'But he could be useful.'

Day after day men came, defeated and ragged, and lined up with their applications in hand. It was not always O'Connor interviewing them, but he looked over every application. And after two days he got rid of Schultz, who was useless. He claimed everyone was 'a good man'. Gruber seemed conscientious at least. There were different people in the selection meeting every day: usually a German policeman, that is, Gruber or somebody else, then O'Connor, Owen, one of the enlisted men, preferably an MP.

One day, O'Connor noticed that Gruber spent a long time with one particular application. Gruber passed the application to the other German, a former assistant chief, who also reacted to the application. 'What have you got there?' said O'Connor and held out his hand. Gruber hesitated and then passed it to the lieutenant.

'What's special about this one?'

Gruber hesitated again.

'Was he a Nazi?' O'Connor asked.

'Yes, sir. This man is trouble.'

The other German nodded in agreement.

O'Connor looked to Owen and Veroni. He switched to English. 'Do either of you guys remember this guy?' He looked at the application. 'Geismeier? Willi Geismeier?'

'Wait. Was he the skinny guy with the thick glasses?' said Sergeant Owen. 'This guy spoke perfect English. Remember?'

'Oh, yeah. That's right.'

'So, he's a Nazi?' said O'Connor to Gruber. 'Was he high up in the Party? Do you know?

'Maybe. A criminal in any case,' said Gruber.

'OK,' said O'Connor. 'The MPs have to pick him up.'

'There's no address on the application. He left almost everything blank. So how do we pick him up?' said Veroni.

'We put him on the list of hires,' said O'Connor. 'When he shows up for work, the MPs are waiting.'

WILLI GEISMEIER

Willi arrived as instructed at police headquarters for his first day of work, only to be arrested by four American military policemen. If he was surprised, he didn't show it.

'Take him to the brig,' said Major Becker.

'Wait a minute, Major,' said Lieutenant O'Connor. 'Give me some time with this guy, would you?'

'Why?'

'Something's not quite right,' he said. O'Connor couldn't say what it was, but something about Gruber's reaction had seemed off, and seeing the guy now, well, it just felt wrong.

'OK, Lieutenant. Ten minutes.'

The major and the MPs went outside and lit up cigarettes.

'Have a seat, Mr Geismeier. I understand you speak English.'

'I do,' said Willi.

'How is that?' said the lieutenant.

'Many years ago, I was a student of English literature. Shakespeare in particular.'

'Really? Did you spend time in England?'

'I spent two summers in London doing research at the British Museum.'

'When was that?'

'Before the first war.'

'Do you know why you were arrested just now?'

'No.'

'Were you ever a member of the Nazi Party?'

'No.'

'Never?'

'Never.'

'And yet, I have reliable information that you *were* a Nazi, and an active one with some rank in the Party. How do you explain that?'

'My experience has taught me, Lieutenant, that when one says "reliable information" or other phrases like that, it often means that the information isn't reliable at all. If I had to guess where your reliable information comes from, I'd guess it was one or more of my former police colleagues. Am I right?'

Lieutenant O'Connor had been caught off guard. He gave Willi a long, hard look. 'You were part of the Munich police department? Is that what you're saying?'

'Yes,' said Willi.

'You didn't say so on your application, or to the officers interviewing you.' O'Connor didn't like being surprised this way.

'No, I didn't. They didn't ask, and it was long ago. I left the department fifteen years ago, before Hitler was Chancellor, and have been a laborer ever since then.'

'Why did you leave the department?'

'I had been suspended once, and I was about to be arrested.'

'That would be when?' said Lieutenant O'Connor.

'1932,' said Willi.

'And you were about to be arrested for . . .?'

'I don't know what the charges would have been, but it was serious. I had been in pursuit of a well-connected murderer. He had friends in the police force.'

'Well connected how?'

'He was an elected NSDAP member of the Reichstag, and he had friends throughout the ranks of the Munich police.'

O'Connor snorted. 'This is really a fabulous story, Mr Geismeier.'

'Everything I told you is in the police records, Lieutenant.'

'The records, which were right downstairs, have all been conveniently destroyed, Mr Geismeier. I suppose you know that.'

'My last job,' said Willi, 'was in police records, Lieutenant, and I'm not surprised they have been destroyed.'

'So, it's pretty convenient, isn't it? For you, I mean?'

'Listen, Lieutenant. I'm not an idiot. I've been at this a lot longer than you have. I wouldn't have brought it up if I didn't have proof of what I just told you.'

'You mean you made copies of police records?'

'No. Not copies. I have the originals. As I said, I worked downstairs, and I took what I needed.'

'You stole police records.'

'I did, Lieutenant. I saw it as part of my job.'

'Your job?'

'To catch criminals, Lieutenant. That was my job.'

Lieutenant O'Connor called Major Becker back in and asked
Willi to tell his story again. 'I'll be damned,' said the major. 'Where
are the records now?'

'At my home,' said Willi.

Major Becker, Willi, and Lieutenant O'Connor drove in a jeep
through the rubble-strewn streets of Munich past Neuhausen-
Nymphenburg, Moosach in the direction of Dachau. They turned
west on Ludwigsfelderstraße then past the rail yards torn up by
bombs. They threaded their way through Untermenzing. What was
left of shipping depots and warehouses gave way to potato and
wheat fields.

'This better be good, Geismeier,' said the lieutenant. They had
been driving half an hour.

'Turn left here,' said Willi. It was a dirt track that led through
a small wood. Beyond the wood they stopped in front of a concrete
hangar with a steel door big enough to drive a truck through. It
was a warehouse that had once belonged to Geismeier Ceramics.
You could still make out the name on the side in faded blue paint.
The large steel door had a smaller door in the middle, and they
went in through that. It was empty inside except for a bicycle
leaning against the wall by the door. At the back of the building
another door led to a small apartment. 'You live here, Geismeier?'
said the lieutenant.

'I do now,' said Willi. 'Before this I pretty much kept moving.'

Willi had been on the run for the last thirteen or so years,
scavenging a life where he could find it, working odd jobs in
Munich, but elsewhere too when he had to leave. He repaired
bicycles in his nephew's shop. He collected scrap and sold it. He
picked up and moved when the SS got interested in him again.
He still had friends in the police, and they kept him apprised of
the situation.

Willi got about by bicycle. He slept in garden sheds and country
houses when they were offered. Benno von Horvath and, after
he was gone, Margarete welcomed Willi for a meal whenever he
could manage it. Others helped too, all of them at great risk to
themselves. You never knew who was going to have the courage.
Bergemann was steadfast. And Fedor Blaskowitz, the Latin
teacher, hid Willi in his tiny apartment more than once at great
risk to himself.

'You don't owe me anything,' said Willi.

'I owe it to myself,' said Fedor. He did not survive the war.

The SS only stopped pursuing Willi once the Americans crossed the Rhine. They had other things to worry about now. For the first time in years Willi could stay in one place, which turned out to be the old Geismeier Ceramics plant.

A door next to Willi's apartment led downstairs to a concrete bunker, now a storage room with a table in the center and cabinets around the four sides of the room. Willi opened a drawer and took out a folded sheet of paper. He unfolded it onto the table. 'This is a map of the Munich police in 1933 when Adolf Hitler came to power,' he said. 'The numbers by the names are file numbers, files that are in these drawers.'

'All these drawers have files in them?' said Lieutenant O'Connor, looking around.

'Holy Christ,' said Major Becker.

Willi turned back to the map and pointed. 'Here is Detective Sergeant Hermann Gruber.' No one had told him that Gruber was Willi's accuser, but based on what he had heard about Lieutenant O'Connor's 'reliable source', Willi thought he knew. And now, so did the Americans.

THE AMERICAN CEMETERY

No matter how long you live, early childhood memories stay with you, even after other memories fade. For instance, Maria Christine recalled with great clarity a children's playground in the Parc Monceau in Paris. All she had to do was close her eyes and she could feel the swing's steel seat and rough ropes in her small hands. She could hear the sound of the children playing. She was five when they left. She also remembered sitting on a hard wooden bench between her mother and father on a long train ride that seemed to go on all night, then being on a boat on rough seas. She was the only one who wasn't sick. The wind had tossed salt spray in her face, and that had made her laugh.

She remembered her father and his pure joy. Until she was an old lady she remembered him holding her high over his face smiling up at her, like the sun. She remembered sitting by his side while he was drawing his famous pictures of New York: women hanging clothes from their tenement windows, Bowery flophouses, soldiers on leave lounging on the stoop. Maria Christine was thirteen when Maximilian went away in an army uniform, a forty-eight-year-old infantry private, and then fourteen when word came that he had died on Omaha Beach. She especially remembered that pain because, in fact, it never went away.

Maximilian's last minute was the longest of his life, longer maybe than all the years until then put together. He lay on his back on the sand, seeing only the clouds overhead. He did not hear anything even though there were men shouting and shells exploding all around him. He did not exactly think of Sophie or Maria Christine, but he felt them there beside him, on top of him, under him, embracing him. He felt them in the rippled sand he lay on, in the salty water lapping at his head and shoulders.

Early in their life on the Lower East Side of New York, Sophie and Maximilian received a letter from Munich. It was written in English in a careful sloping hand on airmail stationery. The postage stamp had Hitler on it.

15 May 1938
Dear Mrs Auerbach and Mr Wolf,

   I hope this finds you and your daughter well. I am no longer in police service, but rather have been earning my living as a laborer. I do all sorts of manual labor. I prefer work that takes me outdoors.

   I am writing to let you know that Otto Bruck, the second man behind the bombing that injured you so grievously, Mrs Auerbach, is dead. He was a Nazi and a vicious criminal (is that redundant?) and was serving (if that is the word) in the Reichstag. He was shot dead by the grieving husband of another of his victims.

   The husband, Ludwig Marschach, a police sergeant, was tried and sent to a prison camp that was recently constructed out near Dachau. I do not know his fate beyond that. I still have a connection or two within the Munich police, but they provide me with information at their peril.

   If I can be of service to you in any way, please send a letter addressed to Karl Juncker at Tullemannstraße 54, Munich.

   Sincerely yours,
   Willi Geismeier

Sophie replied to Willi in German, thanking him for telling her about Otto Bruck and Sergeant Marschach, telling him a little about their life in New York, and asking if he knew anything about Elizabeth Grynbaum. Sophie had written to Elizabeth but had not had an answer. Willi wrote back that he had been able to discover that Elizabeth Grynbaum had recently celebrated her ninetieth birthday and was still living in her same apartment. She still gave music lessons, and had a great-granddaughter, a university student, living with her and looking after her.

   Willi and Sophie continued to correspond occasionally until 1940 when mail to Europe was interrupted and suspended. Ships carrying mail were torpedoed and sunk, and post offices were bombed. Willi stopped hearing from Sophie, and she and Maximilian stopped hearing from him. Then, when she thought she would never hear anything again, Sophie received a short letter.

January 26, 1946
Dear Sophie and Maximilian,
    I will keep this short. I don't know whether it will find its
way to you. Please write and tell me if you get this. I hope
you, Sophie, Maximilian, and Maria Christine are all well.
    Elizabeth Grynbaum was transported to Auschwitz
sometime in late 1944. Her son and his family had been
transported earlier. Frau Grynbaum was nearly 100
and frail, and one can only hope that she did not survive
the trip.
    I am well. I was recently hired by the Munich police
department as a detective.
    Sincerely yours,
    Willi Geismeier

Willi received a reply two weeks later, a long letter that began
with Maximilian's death. Maria Christine, Sophie explained, had
her father's artistic gift. She was sixteen years old and drew
beautifully and was already an accomplished photographer.

Sophie had been working as a journalist for the last five years,
first as a freelance reporter for the *Herald*, and then as a political
reporter for the *New York Times* covering the American election
of 1944. Now, she wrote, she had just gotten an assignment from
Life Magazine to go to France and do a story on the Normandy
American Cemetery and Memorial at Omaha Beach. She had
persuaded *Life* to hire Maria Christine as the photographer. The
editors had looked through Maria Christine's pictures. 'They're
terrific,' said the pictures editor. 'No denying that, but she's sixteen.
She's just a girl.' The editor might have had a point if he hadn't
said, 'She's just a girl.'

'Her father's buried there,' Sophie told the editor. 'My husband
and her father.'

'So, Willi,' Sophie wrote, 'Maria Christine and I are going to
France. Visiting Maximilian's grave means more to us than words
can describe.

'We land in Le Havre June fourth and from there a driver
will take us to Omaha Beach where we will spend two days,
including the second anniversary of the landing and of Maximilian's
death.

'I don't think I could set foot in Europe without visiting Munich.

I dread this visit and yet yearn for it. It would please me greatly if we could meet then. Would that be possible?'

On the morning of June 9, 1946, Willi was at his desk working on a case in which a so far unidentified German had killed an American GI. According to treaty, the case came under American jurisdiction. But the Americans had asked that Willi be part of the investigation.

'Geismeier,' the desk sergeant popped his head in the door, 'you have a visitor.'

'I'll be right out, Sergeant.' Willi put together the files he had been working on and slid them into a drawer so that the top of his desk was bare. Then he opened another drawer and took out two bunches of flowers. He looked in the mirror by the door and adjusted his tie, which was something Willi Geismeier almost never did.

Sophie and Maria Christine stood up as he came out into the waiting room. Willi and Sophie looked at one another for a long minute. Maria Christine couldn't help herself. She took a picture.

AUTHOR'S NOTE

I n a historical novel, such as this, one hangs a story on a historical framework and then takes liberties along the way. The object is to do this all seamlessly so that fact and fiction become indistinguishable, offering a clearer and deeper view than facts by themselves can afford.

Some of the language Hitler uses in this book is, despite its currency, taken from his actual speeches. His most clownish behavior also happened. He really did jump on a table in a beer hall and fire a pistol into the ceiling to begin his Putsch. And he scurried away like a frightened crab the next day when the Putsch was put down.

A more important historical part of this book, and one that surprised me, is the story of the *Munich Post* newspaper. The real *Munich Post* sounded the alarm about Hitler, calling him out as a thug and criminal through the thirteen or so years of his rise.

When Hitler took power in 1933, one of his first acts was to shut down the paper, arresting reporters and editors, and sending them to the recently opened camp in nearby Dachau, where many of them were tortured and killed. It is even true, as unlikely as it sounds, that Hitler then had the presses hauled off and melted down. He even had the house number of the building suppressed forever, so savage was his hatred.

News reporters are under attack again around the world. They are being disparaged as 'enemies of the people.' They are arrested, harassed, and killed for reporting the news. The news media – television, radio, print, internet – are the main instrument of our liberty. We allow their suppression at our peril.